TI

PER JACOBSEN

STRUNG III

THE LAST DROP

STRUNG III: THE LAST DROP

Copyright © 2022
Per Jacobsen & HumbleBooks
1st edition, 2022

Cover Art: Per Jacobsen

ISBN: 978-87-94319-06-5

This book is dedicated to my wife,

Sarah Jacobsen.

If you know her, you know why.

If not, then I hope that you have

found light in your life in other ways.

part 1

THE RESEARCH CENTER

"But what if the chubby guy on the track is your wife?"
—O. E. Geralt, Philosopher, Officer.

chapter 1

From the large billboard in front of the entrance to the FullCart supermarket in Hollowfolk, three people hang. Halfway dissolved and all the way dead. Three human beings, which no one in the last two years has cared enough about to cut down and give a proper burial.

However, one of them—a man dressed in an apron with the same yellow and blue colors as the supermarket logo on the building behind him—has at this very moment reached the end of his hanging time.

Maybe it's the rope, or maybe it's his neck bones finally giving in. At any rate, he suddenly falls down to the ice-covered sidewalk.

The impact causes both of the man's kneecaps to

crunch and slide out, while his lower legs shoot out to each side.

In so random a coincidence that one would almost think the dead man has planned it, he hits the curb the exact second that a vehicle stops in front of the supermarket. The first vehicle in a very long time.

A viewer with a penchant for superstition might have wondered if there was some invisible force left in the dead man's body. A will that drove him to let go at that very moment because he wanted to be noticed one last time.

If so, it's in vain. The only thing the two people in the small truck offer the dead man on the sidewalk—and his comrades still hanging from the sign—is a look as brief as it is devoid of interest.

Even when one of them accidentally bumps his foot against the man's twisted leg on his way to the supermarket entrance, it doesn't make much of an impression. He doesn't even slow down to see what it was. He just walks on as if nothing happened.

The two men from the truck—presumably the only ones within miles who still have a pulse—are

Randall Morgan and David Pearson.

And they haven't always been as cynical and apathetic as they are now.

Randall was once what some would call a *soft* man. He was a father and semi-famous author.

But that was a long time ago. These days, his fingertips touch the trigger of his Smith & Wesson far more often than they touch a keyboard, and his son isn't his son anymore. He's a monster.

No, Billy is not *a* monster. He's *the* monster. The merciless leader of the army of murderous children who were behind the massacre at the Redwater football stadium.

Randall's companion, David, is also a completely different person than he once was. Before the fall of civilization, he was an ordinary teenager with ordinary teenage problems, such as surviving the next lunch break or the next class without embarrassing himself.

Now he has survived both his parents, all his schoolmates ... and Rose, who could very well have become the love of his life.

Rose was one of the victims of the massacre in

Redwater.

One of the many whom Billy got killed.

The rubber moldings under the entrance doors squeal loudly as Randall shakes them free of ice and snow and pushes the doors aside.

Even after such a long time—about two years—there is still a second where his brain expects that he will be met with a gush of hot air when he enters the supermarket.

Of course, that doesn't happen. Because it's just as cold inside the store as it is outside.

There isn't any light in the ceiling lamps above them either, but at least the large glass panes in the facade allow a good portion of daylight to get through. Enough to keep them from having to turn on the flashlights.

Before stepping in between the grocery racks, both Randall and David stop and spend a few seconds studying the room. Then they exchange a glance and a nod, after which they each enter their passage.

On the actual grocery shelves, there's nothing but dust to be found, but that's no surprise. For the same reason, they don't waste a lot of time skimming the shelves before they both get on their knees and lean all the way down to the floor so they can look under the racks.

On Randall's side, there's a treasure—two cans of cocktail sausages and a bag of fried onions—and he can hear David pulling something out on his side as well.

"Fuck yeah, spaghetti," David says right after, and Randall feels a faint smile growing in the corners of his lips. Before the apocalypse, he would most likely not have believed it if someone told him that spaghetti would be among the first and worst shortages. On that matter, however, he has become considerably wiser.

After double-checking the floor under the racks, they get up and move farther into the store.

On the right side there are freezing and cooling units all the way along the back wall, but they don't even bother to check those. They have made that mistake before, and you only have to fill your nostrils once with the stench of fish and vegetables that haven't been on ice for months before the lesson is learned.

What does catch their interest, though, is the red door to the right of the cash register. Three things make it interesting: It's made of metal, it has a padlock on it that—amazingly—is still intact, and on the wall above it hangs a sign with the word *STORAGE* printed on it.

Randall and David exchange a look and then both gaze back at the padlock with narrowed eyes.

"There was a car repair shop across the road," Randall says, pointing to the window in the facade. "Maybe there's something over there we can use to break open the lock?"

David nods.

"Can you do that? I'll check out the rest in here, and maybe the back alley, in the meantime."

"Deal. You holler if there's anything."

With those words, Randall turns around and walks back to the entrance doors.

Stepping out between them, he is blinded by the bright light of the morning sun, which is reflected in the snow and shoots up at him from several different angles. It burns and most of all feels as if someone has thrown a handful of coarse salt in his eyes.

He holds his hand up in front of his face and stands still, letting his eyes get used to the light. He then shifts his gaze over to the buildings across the street.

A clothing store whose windows have been smashed so the three naked mannequins behind it now stand knee-deep in snow, a dirty laundromat ... and then the building which is of interest to him. The car repair shop.

He starts walking over there and once again strokes the hanged man from the billboard with his foot. But still, the sight of a dried-up corpse neither shocks nor impresses Randall. He just glances at it for a split second, then sniffles and moves on.

There is, however, something that makes him stop when he's halfway across the snow-covered street.

For a moment he doubts his senses, because it is a bit windy, and this causes small clouds of snow to rise, rushing across the street, disturbing his vision. Besides, there is the possibility that it could be from an animal.

But no, after studying them a moment longer, the matter is settled: the footprints in the snow do not belong to an animal. They belong to a human being.

Two thoughts, both relating to his traveling companion, run through Randall's head. The first is whether the footprints might be David's, but the answer to that comes as quickly as the question is asked. For neither he nor David would be capable of squeezing their feet into shoes that small.

The next question—whether he ought to call his partner out here—requires a bit more reflection, but he also ends up with a no. None of the footprints lead towards the supermarket, so there is no immediate threat to David. Moreover, there is only one set of tracks, so it's not a group.

With that reasoning, Randall continues straight ahead until he's reached the car repair shop.

Of the two garage doors in the workshop entrance, one is sufficiently open for him to enter, if he crouches. Behind it he finds the actual repair shop—a large room divided into two sections with a half-wall, made of stacked car tires.

Both sections have a car lift, but there are no cars on them. There are plenty of loose spare parts scattered across the workbench by the back wall, though.

He walks closer and skims the table. A box of rubber hoses of different sizes, a bunch of oil-smeared rags, and an exhaust pipe that has never been taken out of the plastic wrapping it was delivered in, as well as a bunch of smaller parts he doesn't know the names of.

Behind the table, a large metal board is mounted on the wall. On it hangs a wide selection of tools and an old calendar in which a young woman in a bikini washes the windshield of a black Chevrolet.

The woman is gorgeous, but it's other things on the calendar page that steal Randall's focus. Because the name of the month, *October*, serves as an eerie reminder that this was when the world came to a standstill two years ago ... and then there is the car. For the black Chevrolet in the photo is exactly the same model as the one Randall's big brother owned.

However, Tommy's Chevrolet is never going to look like its twin from the calendar again. That would be a miracle, since Tommy's Chevy was wrecked for good when two patrol cars—deliberately—torpedoed it and threw it laterally into the entrance of Newcrest Memorial Hospital ... where it, incidentally, is still stuck.

But then again, what would be the purpose of fixing that car? Tommy is also gone. It was the first visible order Billy gave when he finally showed his true colors that day at the football stadium in Redwater.

For a second, Randall is back to that day. For a second, before his inner eye, he sees Billy standing up on the handicap platform. Watches him raise his hand against the rugged clouds of the thunder-gray sky, then slam it downward like a judge's hammer. A simple but fateful motion that triggered the bullet which, in the following second, buried itself in Tommy's neck.

Randall senses the small—and by now well-known—signs of an incipient panic attack: dryness in his mouth, his chest tightening, a galloping pulse, and he closes his eyes.

One ... two ... three deep breaths. A little better.

He opens his eyes again and makes sure to keep his gaze over on the left side of the tool board, so it doesn't find the calendar again.

There are several things on the board that could easily handle the task, but his choice falls on a large wrench. It should be able to wrest or knock the shackle of the padlock free so they can find out what goodies FullCart's storage room has to offer.

After pulling it down from the board, he glances at the wrench for a moment, rotating it in his hand. Then he nods and starts walking back toward the open garage door. However, he doesn't take many steps before he halts once more.

Outside the gate, he can see his own footsteps in the snow. Across them runs another set of tracks. They are the same size as the ones he saw earlier, but this time they run in the opposite direction.

Someone has moved past the gate out in the street while he was standing with his back turned.

He considers pulling his Smith & Wesson out from his pants but decides not to and tightens his grip on the wrench instead.

With the tool in his hand and his shoulder pulled back, he makes his way out through the shop's gate, turns left, and follows the unknown footprints.

He moves slowly, getting more tense with each step, but at the same time stubbornly intent on unraveling the mystery, on finding the owner of the prints and clarifying whether he or she is a threat. Also, it cannot be postponed, as he then runs the risk of the tracks being eaten by the snow.

The same snow makes him cringe and curl when the wind occasionally swirls fistfuls of loose flakes up, hitting his cheeks. It's incredible that such a thin layer of tiny ice crystals can make his skin feel like it's about to burn off his face.

The tracks lead him farther down the street, far enough that the FullCart sign and the two bodies hanging from it have almost disappeared behind a white fog as he looks back over his shoulder. But then the tracks turn left, into a narrow alley between two buildings.

And halfway through the alleyway, they stop

abruptly in front of a door that is ajar.

That's a bad idea, Randall.

The thought is his own, but the voice he hears in his head belongs to his ex-wife, Allie. That's nothing new, though. She's been hiding somewhere inside of his head for years, and she rarely shuns a chance to throw a scornful comment into the mix or share her opinion if he's about to make a questionable decision.

Sometimes he listens to her. But not this time.

He stops in front of the door and stands still for a moment, listening.

There's a faint hiss, which may just be from an open window somewhere in there. Otherwise, nothing.

He takes a breath and then gently pushes the door with the tip of his boot.

The door swings open, revealing a narrow hallway, which, apart from a mirror and a shoe cabinet, is completely empty. At the end of it is another door. This one is wide open, and behind it is a large, semi-dark room, the contents of which instantly reveal that this building once housed a clothing store.

The room is chock-full of clothes racks, mannequins, and exhibition tables, all covered in a thick layer of dust.

He can smell it, too. It hangs in the air, like a suffocating swarm of tiny insects seeking to pass through his mouth and nostrils. Dust particles and disintegrating fabric.

A faint creak, presumably from a loose board in the wooden floor, sounds somewhere ahead, confirming what he already knows: he's not alone.

"Is anyone here?" he tries without the slightest expectation of getting an answer. And he doesn't get one ... unless, of course, one considers the sound suddenly dying out a form of response.

Though he tries, it's hard to ignore the creeping unease in his mind that becomes more and more intrusive as he moves forward between the dusty clothes racks and the disquieting, faceless mannequins.

He knows it's his overactive imagination—what his ex-wife always used to call his *twisted writer's brain*—that is to blame, and that he shouldn't listen to it. The problem is, though, that it can be awfully convincing, and right now it strongly insists that one of these mannequins could easily decide to reach for him with its long, white, plastic fingers. Maybe even close them around his neck and—

Pull yourself together! he orders himself while shaking his shoulders and neck as if trying to jumpstart himself somehow.

He goes on, anxious and dangerously aware that *he* is now the one revealing his presence with the sound of creaking floorboards under the soles of his boots.

At the end of the narrow passage between the clothes racks and the white plastic people there is about three feet of free floor space, illuminated by a window in the wall behind it. And there, in the light, across two of the floorboards, lie two thin streaks of water. Both are curvy, and together they draw the distinctive outline of a shoe sole. Same size as the footprints that led him in here.

And the angle tells him that the shoe's owner must have turned right at this spot.

He gathers courage for a moment, then tightens

his grip on the wrench and walks forward until he reaches the end of the passage. Then he turns right … and stops so suddenly that one would think he had collided with an invisible barrier.

No, not that, he thinks, although the size of the footprints had warned him in advance that it might be a possibility. *Anything but that.*

The girl isn't very big, and the way she is crumpled up in the corner only adds to that impression.

She's also thin, almost what one would call *scrawny*. The wrist that sticks out of the sleeve of her brown jacket isn't much thicker than the hanger bars on the clothes racks around them, and the cheekbones under her wide-open puppy eyes protrude so clearly it looks like they're on the verge of bursting through the skin.

She could have been a character from an Oliver Twist novel.

Turn around, Allie whispers in the back of Randall's head with a voice that sounds just as upset as he feels. *Turn around, go back, get David and drive away from here, without looking back and without saying a word about this. And if he asks what took you so long, lie. Say that it dragged out because the garage door into the shop was stuck.*

Part of Randall wants to do just that. Listen to the inner, distorted version of his ex-wife and just walk away.

Ignore the child.

But.

He's made that mistake before, and it cost him dearly. It cost them *all* dearly. Tommy, Rose, the Mayor ... hell, almost everyone in both San Hiva and the Redwater camp paid the ultimate price because he made that very mistake. Because he ignored the child.

So deep down, he knows what it actually is he's facing, and he knows what he ought to do.

But the girl's green eyes are wide open and terrified, and the locks sticking out from under her knitted hat reveal that her hair is red.

Just like Rose's hair.

Now she makes a strained swallowing motion and blinks so the puppy eyes don't dry out. Then she slowly begins to raise one hand up protectively in front of her. Almost as if she's also aware what it is he's trying to muster up the courage to do—and wants to tell him that he shouldn't.

That he should spare her instead.

It's the same pale hand as before—the one with the hanger-bar wrist—and he realizes it's the only one he's seen. That her other hand has been behind her back the whole time.

Barely has he been hit by this realization before the girl jumps up, letting out a horrific scream, after which she throws herself at him.

Her hand isn't hidden behind her back anymore. Neither is the knife.

It looks like a utility knife, but he's not a hundred percent sure, as she swings it so quickly and frantically from side to side that it forms a semi-transparent, yellow infinity sign in the air in front of her.

At the last second, he manages to swing the wrench up in front of him so the knife hits it, rather than the artery in his thigh.

Meeting the metal of the wrench causes the blade of the utility knife to break off and fly in between the clothes racks, where it hits the floor with a clink.

However, the delay is short-lived, for the girl doesn't hesitate to push the slider up, making a fresh blade appear at the end of the grip.

"Stop, for God's sake," he tries. "I don't want to hurt you!"

It's no use. Her body makes her look like a ten- or eleven-year-old girl, but the hatred in her eyes is so intense and so deep that it must have taken much longer to develop. The likelihood that any words from his mouth could quell that hatred has to be almost non-existent.

Still, he needs to try.

"You don't have to do this," he says as he knocks one of the mannequins down onto the floor in front of the girl to create distance between himself and the knife, which once more has started to draw yellow patterns in the air. "Please, I'm begging you."

The girl responds with a sound that is a bizarre mixture between a snake's hiss and a dog's growl. Then she steps—still with the knife dancing from side to side—over the mannequin.

When she's safely past it, the knife suddenly

stops. At the same time, the girl bends her knees slightly, enough for Randall to know what's about to happen. That she's going to leap toward him again.

He takes a step backward, getting ready to dodge. With a little luck, he might even be able to wrest the knife from her if he can knock one of the clothes racks over her so she can't—

Something pulls the thought from him and moves his gaze away from the knife. A movement, a blurry silhouette that has appeared on the other side of the glass of the window in the back wall.

"DAVID, NO!" he yells, but it's too late. The trigger is pulled, and the bullet is sent off. It penetrates first the glass of the window, then the skull of the red-haired girl who looks like a character from Oliver Twist.

She collapses, hits the floor with a muffled bump, and then there is nothing but silence inside the semi-dark room. At least until David sticks his head in through the shattered window and casts a glance at the girl. With eyes that are uncannily cold and almost as hateful as hers were seconds ago.

"Little fucking monsters," he mutters, shaking his head, before looking up at his stunned traveling companion. "So, did you manage to find anything for the padlock?"

chapter 2

In a world where you can no longer take a stroll in any city without encountering hanged people, Randall does realize how it may seem a bit futile, perhaps even bizarre. Nevertheless, there is something driving him to carry the lifeless girl all the way out to the narrow alley from which he entered the building. Out there is a large garbage container, in which he gently lays her down, before he closes its lid.

Not a coffin, not six feet under, but at least some kind of burial ... and that's got to be better than nothing, right?

When the silent ritual is over, he goes back to the supermarket, where David—now armed with the wrench—has just succeeded in breaking open the padlock on the storage door.

"Is there anything good?" Randall asks.

David is standing in the doorway into the storage room, and he has his back to him, so Randall can't see his face. But considering how cold his eyes were earlier, he's not sure that's such a bad thing.

"Well," David finally replies, "there are a few boxes of water. That always comes in handy. And canned ham. Most of the other stuff has expired."

That information had been revealed to Randall beforehand by his nostrils. Even all the way over at the entrance of the supermarket, where he stands, he can smell the mold and the rot that they have unleashed by opening the storage door.

"We'd better get it on the truck," David says, whereafter he goes into the storage room and picks up one of the boxes of water bottles.

Randall opens his mouth with the intention of having a serious talk with his young companion about what just happened ... but then David turns around, and he decides to wait.

David's eyes aren't sad— at least not in any other way than they have been since Redwater and Rose.

They don't show any sign of guilt or shame, either. That's not why Randall remains silent. What makes him postpone the talk is the look of pure exhaustion on David's face.

David doesn't look young anymore. He looks old. His face resembles some kind of matte, grayish rubber mask, the features of which are so washed out with fatigue that it appears as expressionless as the faces of the creepy mannequins from the clothing store.

The silence between them lasts a long time. They take what they can use from the storage room and load it onto the back of the truck without saying a single word to each other. Then they cover the back with the tarp, fasten it, and get into the vehicle—still without exchanging more than a few awkward glances.

But when Randall sits down in the driver's seat and realizes that the wind, and the snow it throws at the truck, are the only sounds he can hear, it suddenly becomes too much.

"You didn't have to kill her," he mumbles, rubbing his hands back and forth on the edge of the steering wheel. "She was a kid."

"You know what she was," David answers indifferently, while pulling the seat belt down across his chest and snapping it into the buckle.

How can he be so damned cynical? Randall thinks, though he knows the answer very well.

David is cynical because he's broken. Because *everything* is broken. Because the miserable world in which he lives is as devoid of mercy as it is of hope. And because it has taken everything from him.

No, Randall, Allie whispers in his thoughts. *There is hope. It's right there, in the glove compartment. If you just make sure to keep your eyes on the ball and bring it to the right place, there is hope.*

The hope she's talking about is a transparent plastic bag containing a quarter liter of a thick, silver-colored liquid, as well as a small, disgusting tadpole-like animal. That very bag once hung from an IV rack in the auditorium at Newcrest Memorial Hospital, where it was connected to his son's veins via a thin rubber hose.

And yeah, the IV bag does represent hope. That's

why he went back to the hospital and picked it up. His intention is to bring the bag to the woman whose name and title are on the business card in his pocket.

HELEN WALKER

SENIOR RESEARCHER; BIOCHEMISTRY A2

ARL RESEARCH CENTER

2100 RAVEN ROAD

ADELPHI, MARYLAND

Randall has only met Helen Walker once—and at the time, he was on the fence because she sought him out and was interested in examining Billy.

But all that was *before* Redwater, and now he's the one who's planning to show up unannounced, hoping that she—with the help of the IV bag's contents—can perhaps shed some light on what happened to Billy and all the other kids.

Deep down, he may also be hoping it could be the key to fixing it.

The key to a cure.

But will it also be a cure for David? And what about you? Can the two of you be fixed as well, or is that a lost cause?

He glances over at the passenger seat where David sits, fiddling with the rubber strip in the frame of the window as he stares indifferently out at the FullCart sign.

"It's not that I don't get it," Randall says. "That you shot her, I mean. I get it. I'm just ... concerned about you. About us."

David meets his gaze but says nothing.

"My point is that I think we have to be careful," Randall says. "That we should at least try to hold on to our ... humanity so we don't become ..."

He hesitates for a long time before finishing the sentence, and when he does, he can barely get the words out.

"So we don't become like them. So that we don't lose the ability to distinguish between what is right and what is wrong."

David continues to stare at him, but the expression in his eyes has changed a tad. Where he before looked apathetic, he now seems annoyed and strangely confrontational.

"Was that the full monologue?" he asks, biting the left side of his frost-cracked lips. "Or do you have any more philosophical nuggets you would like to share before we drive?"

Randall shakes his head, puts the key in the ignition, and turns it.

"No, that was all of it. Thank you for listening."

He tries not to let it shine through, but inside he's relieved by David's provocative response. Because, ironically, David's aggravated expression makes him look more normal than he has in a long time. It makes him look like a teenager looking to piss off a grown-up ... which is, all things considered, better than a burnt-out, eighteen-year-old man who has lost everything.

So maybe there is still hope for the both of them.

chapter 3

A little more than a day later, Randall Morgan and David Pearson find themselves in the same seats in the same vehicle, but the surroundings outside the windows are very different.

There is still plenty of snow, ice, and wind, but where they the day before were enclosed by buildings, they now see only one. It is the concrete building which lies as an extension to the Raven Congress's dam and probably served as a control center for it.

Whether the dam is still able to live up to its subtitle—*hydroelectric power plant*—only God knows, but Randall strongly doubts it. Partly because it doesn't look manned, and partly because some of the reservoir has frozen over.

As he ponders these things, Randall picks up out of the corner of his eye that David is flipping the road map in his hands, smoothing it against his thighs, before lifting it back up.

"Is something wrong?"

Before answering, David glances back and forth a few times between the map and a ravine in the landscape ahead, where the river cuts through a snowy pine forest.

"I can't see the bridge," he says, tilting the map so Randall can see.

The map is one they found at the reception area of an abandoned motel along Highway 97. Actually, it's a tourist map, but aside from a few oversized icons occasionally chewing up a portion of the landscape, eager to show off attractions like a mushroom house and a duck decoy museum, the map is accurate enough to navigate by.

"It has to be that one," Randall says, pointing.

David's gaze moves along the invisible line that Randall's finger draws in the air, ending on the bridge. Then he frowns and says:

"Yeah, figures. What did I expect?"

The bridge is made of timber, and its foundation consists of eight broad beams, cast into two large concrete blocks out in the middle of the river. Under the roadway, these wide beams are connected with many smaller ones, thereby forming four intertwined bases resembling inverted pyramids.

Why David missed the bridge in the first place is not difficult to understand, as nothing about it has been maintained for at least two years, resulting in all the woodwork being overgrown with algae and moss. Along with the snow layer on the top railing, this makes it almost impossible to discern the bridge from the forest landscape behind it.

Upon reaching the bridge, Randall lifts his foot off the pedal until the gauge needle is all the way down at about six miles per hour.

There he lets it balance as the truck rolls out onto the bridge. He doesn't dare go any faster as the roadway appears to be coated with a thick layer of ice—probably the result of a long period of cold, combined with constant splashes of water from the river as it collides with the concrete blocks below. And salting the roads to remove ice hasn't exactly been at the top of anyone's priority list since the world ended.

The bridge creaks disturbingly, but except for one time when the truck slides sideways so the side mirror scrapes against the railing on the right side of the bridge, the ride goes pretty smoothly.

At least in Randall's opinion. David, who suffers from a bad fear of heights, doesn't seem to agree entirely, though. He's pale and only takes his eyes off the map when all four tires are safely over on the other side.

"The road we're on now should be ... yup, it is. Look over there."

Randall looks in the direction David is pointing, reads the two words on the sign, and nods.

RAVEN ROAD.

The finish line is eerily close now, and part of him feels an almost intoxicating excitement at that realization.

However, another part of him feels something else. Something that borders on panic.

As if some invisible force has reached a hand into his mind, pulled out that thought, and sent it over to David, the young man says:

"What do we do if there's no one there? If we find the research center and it's completely empty."

"It's not empty," Randall says with a conviction that he doesn't feel a hundred percent. "*They* came to me, remember? Not the other way around. And that was only three or four months ago."

David nods but doesn't look very convinced.

"A lot can happen in three or four months."

He doesn't elaborate, but there's no need. That one sentence is enough to play a movie to Randall's inner eye. A movie that starts with a valley filled with dead police officers and ends with a football stadium filled with dead friends.

A lot can—quite rightly—happen in a matter of months.

"If anyone is able to get something useful out of that bag, it's them," Randall says. "So, we need to try."

"Mm ... what was the address again?"

Randall takes one hand off the steering wheel and is about to reach for his back pocket when he realizes it's unnecessary. By now, he has spent so much time staring at that business card that the address is burned into his consciousness.

"2100 Raven Road," he says.

David nods.

"Then we just have to figure out where on it we are now."

The answer comes shortly after, when they have come out on the other side of the snowy pine forest, where clusters of buildings lie on both sides of Raven Road. One of the buildings—*Cliffsdale Baptist Church*—has a bronze sign hanging outside with the house number, 2068, engraved.

It also has a dead woman hanging down from the roof of an outdoor bell tower, but that detail Randall only records peripherally.

When they leave the town again, they are only twelve house numbers from their target—and of those twelve they are only able to actually see the numbers of two, as the others are farms, located at the end of dirt roads and large driveways.

Still, neither Randall nor David is in doubt when they reach number 2100.

The obvious indicator is the fence. A large, chain

link fence, about ten feet tall, which at the top has a foot and a half extra that slopes outwards and is sheathed with barbed wire.

The letters *ARL* in the name stand for *Army Research Laboratory*, and few things signal *military property* like such a fence.

"It looks pretty abandoned," David says as Randall stops the truck in front of the entrance gate—a section of the fence that can roll to the side using some small wheels mounted at the bottom, as well as a small electric motor at the top.

And David is right. It does look empty. At least if you follow the cables from the engine and look down at the vacant shed which undoubtedly used to house some annoying guard who always demanded to see identification before he pressed the button.

But Randall isn't looking at the guard shed. His attention is directed to the ground below and around the fence.

"There are people here," he says, pointing. "Look how the snow has sunk a bit here and there."

"As if there are tire tracks that have been covered recently," David says, halfway asking, halfway ascertaining.

Randall nods, then moves his index finger further to the right.

"And then look over there. If the gate wasn't still in use, there wouldn't be a pile of snow where it stops."

David looks and then nods his head up and down in approval. Next, he grabs the handle and opens the door on his side.

After getting out, he walks over to the shed, where he leans in through the glassless window. A moment later, he turns around and shrugs while his lips form the words: *It was worth a shot.*

The wheels squeal loudly under the gate as David grabs ahold and pulls it aside. When the gap is big enough, he signals to Randall, who drives the truck through.

The enclosed area they now find themselves in is large and houses so many buildings that it looks like a small town. There are also a couple of buildings that don't look like houses, but rather a strange fusion between a grain silo and a missile ramp.

These have apparently also caught the attention of David, who points to them as he gets in the truck, sending Randall a questioning look.

"No idea," Randall replies. "And frankly, I'm not sure I want to know either."

As they drive into the passage between the first two buildings, Randall carefully studies the windows. All of them are empty and dark, not showing any signs of life.

Still, he has a nagging feeling that somewhere in there, curious eyes are watching them.

David seems to share that feeling. He keeps looking around and shifting uneasily in his seat at the slightest sound.

At the end of the passage stands a crane. Below it two green containers, both labeled *PROPERTY OF THE U.S. ARMY*, are piled up. To the right of them is another building—a modern, white, and sophisticated one. The kind that in both design and material choice—marble tiles, frosted glass, and stainless steel—emits the same message.

That it is *sterile*.

Randall and David exchange a look and both nod. Then Randall turns the truck to the right and drives toward the building.

He does, however, only get halfway there before the sound of two metallic thumps as the grenades hit the truck—one on the hood, the other on the door on the right—makes him stop.

Two blurry men, uniformed and armed. That's all Randall manages to register before the flash grenades go off and his whole world is reduced to a blinding white.

chapter 4

"Hands on your heads!" a voice roars from some-where in the all-enveloping white universe. "Keep your fucking hands on your head!"

"We are!" David replies in the passenger seat. "We're not ... hey, let go of me!"

"On your knees!" is the only answer he gets.

The next moment, the truck's door is ripped open on Randall's side, and a new voice, deeper and more relaxed than the other, says:

"You too, come on. On your knees."

Randall tries to follow the order, but it's not easy, because even though more colors are now starting to appear on his retina, everything is still so out of focus that he's on the verge of falling as he crawls out of the truck. However, he knows when his knees and hands reach the ground as they get wrapped in biting cold snow.

As he sits there, huddled on the ground with his fingers buried in ice crystals, the owner of the unfamiliar voice manifests as the white overlay filter of the grenades gradually fades from Randall's eyes.

The man starts out as a pair of blurry military boots in front of Randall's hands. Then a green uniform, a rifle, and finally a face joins the picture.

The face is weathered, and a myriad of wrinkles and old scars make the dark brown skin look like bark on the trunk of a coniferous tree. The man looks tough, but in a fair way. The way a soldier should look. Like someone who takes no joy in violence, but who isn't afraid to roll up his sleeves and clench his fists when duty calls.

His partner, standing behind David over on the other side, gives off a completely different vibe. His crooked smile gives the impression of a man who thrives in gray areas, perhaps even one hoping that David is going to try something, so he has an excuse to knock him out with the butt of the rifle.

"You've got ten seconds to explain who you are and what you're doing here," says the first one.

"Randall Morgan and David Pearson. We are looking for Helen Walker. She's a researcher here, and she contacted me a few months ago. We have brought something that we think she'll be very interested in examining. If you mention my name to her, I'm sure she knows who I am."

As he speaks, Randall makes sure not to lift his head too much, hoping that it will signal humility and thus reduce the risk of a kick in the ribs.

"If you'll let me take it out, I've got a business card in my back pocket," Randall says. "It's one she gave me. Then you can see that—"

"You just keep your fucking hands right where they are!" the soldier over at David's side sneers.

"Take it easy, Farley," his mate says. Next, he leans down to Randall. "Which pocket?"

"The right," Randall mutters, still keeping his gaze fixed on his hands, which by now have been turned completely numb by the snow. "It's in the right back pocket."

"Fine. You stay put. No sudden movements. Is

that clear?"

Randall nods, and the soldier walks a few steps forward, coming over beside him. Then he bends down, slides a finger into Randall's back pocket, and pulls the card out.

In the ensuing seconds, there's utter silence, and the temptation to look up is almost unbearable. So is the temptation to free their hands from the snow, just for a moment.

Yet neither Randall nor David does either of those two things. They wait until the guard clears his throat.

"It looks alright," he says, and judging by the shadows on the ground, he then hands the card over to his colleague.

"So, we bring them in?" the colleague asks, upon receiving the card, and Randall is pretty sure it's disappointment he hears in his voice.

It's a good thing he wasn't alone on duty today, I think.

"Yep," the first one replies. "Then Helen can explain what the hell this is."

"Mm," says the disappointed guard—and then

he manages to find a spark of hope to cling to: "Then you better damn well hope she backs up your story, or you're going to regret it."

Randall says nothing. Neither does David.

"On your feet," says the first soldier. "Nice and easy."

Randall nods and tries to push himself up, but his hands are so thoroughly cold that for a moment he is completely unable to move them. It feels like the bones are squeaking and creaking in there. As if they could easily splinter if he uses too much force.

He feels something grab hold of his arm. A second after, he's on his feet.

"Put them on your stomach," the soldier says. "That's one of the first things we taught new recruits in the past when they were going on their first night drill. It's unpleasant, but it works."

Randall follows the suggestion, placing his quivering hands on his stomach.

Unpleasant is a gigantic understatement, to say the least, but the soldier is right. It works.

"Thank you."

"Don't mention it," the soldier replies, making a sweeping motion with his hand, then he tilts the rifle up and down once as a signal for Randall to start moving.

Randall takes a few steps, but then stops.

"There ... um, there's one more thing," he says. "There's a bag in the glove compartment that we would like to bring. It's for her."

"For Helen Walker?"

Randall nods, and the soldier sends a questioning glance over to his mate, who—not surprisingly—responds by groaning and rolling his eyes.

"Damn it, dude. We're going to freeze our asses off out here."

"Just check the bleeding glove box, Farley."

Despite the imminent risk of freezing his ass off, Farley spends an extra moment staring defiantly at his colleague. Next, he marches over to the truck, opens the door, and then the glove compartment.

"Holy shit."

"What?"

Farley raises his hand, which now holds the corner of the IV bag with the silvery liquid.

His mate looks at it and then at Randall.

"Is that what I think it is?"

Randall nods.

"We found it in a hospital. There is still one of those little bastards in it. Not alive, but ..."

"Bullshit!" Farley exclaims. "They emptied out the IV bags. *All* the IV bags. We've searched every fucking hospital throughout Maryland, and not once did we—"

"This wasn't in Maryland," Randall says. "It was in Pennsylvania. In Newcrest. The doctors missed it when they cleared the place because it had fallen to the floor. And I knew this because ..."

"Because it was his son it was connected to," David concludes for him.

Both soldiers look at Randall with the same gaze. One that contains both skepticism and compassion.

He nods.

"I knew the bag would be under a chair on the floor in there. You see, I ... I left it there myself after I freed my son."

The soldier next to Randall stares at him for a

very long time. Then he bites his lower lip and squints his eyes.

"What did you say your name was?"

"I ... um, Randall. My name is Randall."

"Your last name, I mean."

"Morgan."

The fleeting gaze the two soldiers exchange lasts a second at most ... but it's enough to tell Randall that they've heard of someone else with that last name.

That they've heard of Billy.

"I think it's time we go inside," the soldier on Randall's side says, after which he once again tilts the barrel of the rifle up and down.

And this time, Randall follows the order and starts walking.

chapter 5

It turned out that Randall and David's assumption was correct. The building with the sterile, white exterior indeed was the place where the remaining group of scientists from ARL resides.

What they hadn't foreseen, however, is that the building has a hidden back entrance in the form of a freight elevator, which leads down to a part of the research center that is built underground.

That's the first shock: seeing the two sliding doors move aside, exposing the interior of an elevator. In itself, the sight of electric light is a rarity these days, but seeing a functioning lift—knowing what it must take to power it—is an almost surreal experience for Randall.

The next shock hits him as the elevator doors

slide apart the second time, and the soldiers lead them out into a long, well-lit corridor down in the basement. It's the *tidiness*. Everything is spotless, polished, and probably sanitized.

Not once since before the Collapse has Randall seen a place so clean. Not once.

"We're going this way," one of the guards says, nodding toward the left side of the corridor.

Randall starts walking, but he does so with slow, hesitant steps. For there is a part of him that feels an irrational, but quite genuine, fear that this place might not be real at all.

"Where do you get that much power from?"

The guard escorting Randall looks at him with a doubtful look, as if contemplating whether he ought to give that information. Then he shrugs.

"There's a hydroelectric dam not far from here. And you'd be surprised what a bunch of scientists and engineers with nothing but free time on their hands can conjure up."

Randall glances over at David, who tilts his head slightly as if to say *Well, there you go. It's still running.*

On both sides of them, a series of windows glide

by as they walk down the hallway. Most of the rooms behind these—offices and storerooms with glass shelves filled with various chemical bottles—are semi-dark and empty, but a few are lit up. In one of these, a laboratory, two men in white coats are standing, staring at a centrifuge full of test tubes.

At the end of the corridor, the soldiers lead them to the right and into a new hallway. Here there aren't any windows they can look through. Instead, there are three doors. Two of them are ajar, and the last one is closed. This is also the only one of the three that has an external bolt lock that opens and closes using a code panel on the wall.

Randall doesn't like that detail. Especially not given that this is the door at which the soldier stops.

"Didn't you forget to give us our black and white striped jumpsuits first?" David asks in a voice that is purposefully laid-back and light but carries a sharp undertone of sarcasm.

The soldier stares at him, first with confusion in his face, then with dawning comprehension that develops into a smile.

"Don't worry," he says. "It's only a temporary solution. Until we're sure you're not a threat."

"Is this really necessary?" Randall asks, and just then an uncomfortable sense of déjà vu hits him.

He has said these exact same words to a man in uniform before. Just over two years ago, to be more precise. At the time, the question was directed at a police officer who insisted that Randall—who had done nothing wrong—should get in the back seat of the patrol car rather than drive to the police station in his own car.

Naive as he was, Randall of course did what the authority commanded—and the consequence of that decision? The officer beat him up and tried to hang him from a lamppost.

This isn't the same, he says to himself, but it doesn't take away the nagging sensation in his stomach, which only worsens with each number the guard types into the code panel.

Two short beeping sounds, a flash of green, and then the locking bolts get pulled back with a sharp, metallic *clank*.

Behind the door is a small, square room whose

only pieces of furniture are a table in the center and four chairs stacked in one corner.

Randall catches David's gaze, and to his surprise, he sees something in the young man's eyes that he hasn't seen in a very long time.

Ever since Redwater and Rose, David has alternated between being angry, anguished, hateful, and wallowing in grief. But right now, there's something else. Right now, he looks insecure and tense, perhaps even scared.

"They have every right to be careful," Randall whispers to him. "For all they know, we could be full of it."

David looks at him, and the uncertainty in his eyes instantly evaporates. In its place enters an icy indignation.

"Yeah," he says. "You have to be careful not to trust the wrong people. It can be dangerous."

Randall is too baffled to answer. It's not the first time David has lashed out in a similar way, and there's never been any doubt in Randall's mind that the young man does place at least *some* of the responsibility for Billy's actions on him. That David blames him for being blinded by a father's love and therefore not picking up on the warning signs.

But while this snarky remark isn't the first, it does hit harder than any of the others did. Perhaps because it doesn't feel like it's born from David's grief and powerlessness this time, but rather of something even darker. Something that has an underlying drive, a *will*.

Something that feels like *vindictiveness*.

"Grab a chair and take a seat at the table," the soldier says. "Someone will come in to talk to you in a little while."

"Helen Walker?"

"We'll see."

"It's extremely important that we get to talk to Helen Walker."

"We'll see," the soldier repeats in a tone of voice that clearly states that all two-way communication lines are closed for now. Then he exchanges a brief glance and a nod with his colleague, after which they both walk out of the room.

Randall opens his mouth, but a faint head shake from David convinces him to close it again without saying anything.

It's probably for the best. He probably wouldn't have achieved anything more than annoying the guards by asking again.

The soldier closes the door behind him, and out on the other side, they can hear him enter a sequence of numbers into the panel again. Subsequently, there follows the same beeping sounds as before and the same metallic *clank* when the bolts shoot in. Except, of course, that it sounds way more menacing and definitive this time. Like a large gate being slammed shut.

For a while they remain seated in silence, Randall leaning back in his chair with his arms crossed, David with one hand on his chin and the other drumming on the edge of the table.

At one point, though, his fingers abruptly stop, and he turns to Randall.

"When he asked for your last name ..."

Randall nods.

"Yeah, I noticed it too. They've heard about what happened in Redwater ... or at least about Billy."

"Do you think they suspect us of having been a

part of it?"

"Don't know. But if they do, I don't hold it against them. After all, we walked out of there unharmed ... perhaps as the only ones."

For a moment, there's an absent look in David's eyes, as if he is staring straight through the wall. Then he shakes his head like someone who has just woken up from a daydream ... although Randall knows full well that it was more likely the past David was staring into, and that the daydream was a nightmare. Presumably one in which David sits on the stairs inside the Redwater football stadium holding his dead girlfriend's body in his arms.

"Are you okay?"

David shrugs and nods slowly, then resumes his drumming on the edge of the table.

"At least it's warm in here," Randall continues, mostly because the silence feels awkward and uncomfortable. "And they will let us go soon. They just have to realize that we're on the same side. I mean, it would be pretty idiotic of us to give them the IV bag if we weren't. That would be shooting ourselves in the foot, right? And they can see that too."

"Yeah, of course."

David doesn't exactly sound convinced, and for some reason that makes Randall feel a strong urge to keep talking. Maybe it's because of the snappy remark David gave him earlier.

However, before he gets the chance to begin a new monologue, Randall is interrupted by the sound of the lock, which once again is turned off on the other side of the door. Right after, the door opens and two people step in.

It is not the guards from before, but rather a man and a woman. Unlike the soldiers, this man is not wearing a uniform, just a light brown sweater and a pair of jeans. Still, Randall doesn't doubt for a second that he is military and that he ranks higher than the guards. He exudes, both in posture and motion, authority.

He thought the same about the woman standing next to the man when he first met her—and it still holds true. The tough *no time for goofing around* look in her brown eyes—which may well be a necessary result of having to survive in a male-dominated profession without a Y chromosome—is still there. So is its counterpart, the disarming smile, which is just as hard for Randall not to return now as it was then.

A dangerous but effective combination, those two traits.

"Mr. Morgan," she says, locking her hazel-brown gaze on him. "I have to admit I was surprised to hear that you showed up on our doorstep. The last time we talked, you were … shall we say a bit defensive?"

"I was protecting my son from strangers. You can't really blame me for that, can you?"

For a moment, Walker looks as if she's about to throw back a snide answer, but then she takes a breath, sets an unruly lock of her blond hair back in place behind her ear, and puts on an empathetic, almost mournful facial expression.

"I'm sorry to hear what happened to him," she says. "Of course, we don't know all the details, but we've heard about what happened in Redwater and many other places. All those camps with innocent people. It's … terrible."

Even now, with all that has happened, it's hard for Randall to resist the impulse to defend his child. He feels like hammering a fist into the table and yelling that it wasn't Billy who did all that stuff. That the ... *thing* that pushed Rose to her death from the handicap platform and then gave the signal initiating a heartless massacre was not Billy. That it was something else. A monster that controls his body.

But it's no use. He can twist and turn it as much as he wants. It won't change the fact that it's Billy's hands that hold the conductor's baton for the cruel and murderous army of children. For some reason he's the one they listen to. The one who gives them orders ... and therefore, for any outsider, Billy's face will be the symbol of evil.

"But maybe there's hope," Walker continues. "The gift you brought us today is worth its weight in gold. My colleague is already looking at it. With a bit of luck, the contents of that bag can fill in the last holes of the jigsaw puzzle we've been trying to solve for the past few years."

"A jigsaw puzzle?"

Instead of answering, Walker turns to face the man she was with when she entered the room.

"Can I take them down to the lab? It's easier if they see it."

The man crosses his arms and runs his tongue over his teeth behind his upper lip, causing it to bulge out. Then he nods slowly.

"It's your ass that's on the line if it turns out to be a bad idea."

"As if that's anything new," she says, turning back toward the table. "What do you say we take a little tour?"

chapter 6

"Fucking gross."

The words come from David's mouth, and what they describe is the contents of the row of glass jars that stand on the long table on one side of the lab.

And he's right. They really are gross, the small, tadpole-like animals that are fastened to slanted plates with microscopic needles behind the glass of the jars, as if they were stuffed butterflies.

"No, they aren't pretty," Walker agrees. "But they're vital to us. If we can figure them out, humanity may still have a chance."

"What little remains of us," David bitterly replies, but both Randall and Walker choose to ignore it.

"UPP parasite?" Randall reads aloud from one of

the labels on the jars.

Walker nods.

"That's our temporary umbrella term for them. The U stands for *unidentified*, it's pretty self-explanatory. The two P's stand for *prepubescent*. They've been given that name because all types have in common that they only bind themselves to children who haven't reached puberty yet."

"All types?"

"They seem alike, but we've discerned that there are five individual types of parasites, each of which has its own role and function," Walker says, waving them along. "It's easier to understand if you see the MRIs. Come with me."

She leads them past the table with the glass jars and into a passage between two racks holding various laboratory equipment. At the end of it is a door with her name and title attached.

DR. HELEN WALKER.

SENIOR RESEARCHER, BIOCHEMISTRY.

Behind the door is an office that stands in stark contrast to the well-organized lab. There are stacks of paper and folders on the desk, yellow post-it notes hanging on the side of the filing cabinet, and two pieces of clothing lying on the armrest of a chair—right below a coat rack on the wall.

"Just a sec," Walker says as she rummages through one of the folders. "Here you are."

She takes out a picture of a scan and spins around, after which she turns on a light board on the wall and hangs it up.

The picture is of the unmistakable shape of a human brain. Except that there are five white, drop-shaped spots that stand out.

"This is from a boy we found in a hospital in Silver Spring," Walker says as she once again bends down to the folder and pulls out another picture. "And this is a girl from a hospital in Clinton."

She hangs the picture next to the first one, and while Randall really isn't that surprised, he hears himself gasp. Because it's one thing to imagine how these tiny, repulsive parasites have infected the children's bodies. It's quite another thing to see it illustrated in such a concrete way.

"I could show you many more," Walker says. "But I think you get the point."

"They're all ... the same?" David says, halfway questioning, halfway stating.

"In terms of number and placement, yes," Walker replies. "All the host bodies have had the same five parasites pumped into their veins, and the five parasites have ... attached themselves to the exact same places in their brain. Connected themselves to the same centers, you might say."

"But why?" Randall asks. "What is it they want?"

Walker hesitates a while before answering—and when she does, her brown eyes take on a dash of frustration.

"They want to live forever," she says. "It's that simple. And they've found the key to doing it. Unfortunately for humanity, it's us ... or rather *our offspring*, they need to do it."

"I don't get it," David says. "Why choose kids? Wouldn't it make more sense if they had stayed with stronger hosts? Like in the beginning, when they used the cops."

"I get where you're coming from," Walker replies, nodding. "Big, strong, and *armed* policemen. The problem is that it wouldn't work. Somehow, the parasites are able to stop cell degeneration in the human body, so the host doesn't age and only needs a minimal amount of food to function. But apparently, they can only do it if the host hasn't entered puberty yet."

She hesitates a little, then adds: "Personally, I don't believe that these parasites were what drove the police force. But even if that was the case, I'm not convinced that the officers are in fact stronger hosts, from a psychological standpoint. After all, most people will find it easier to fire a weapon if the bullet is aimed at a murderous cop than if the target is a child."

Randall nods, feeling a chill at the memory of the little girl in Hollowfolk. The memory of how her anxious face made him hesitate even though he knew what he ought to do. And how that same face contracted, making her look like a rabid animal, as she pulled out the utility knife and threw herself at him.

"Can they be removed?" he asks, though not sure if he's able to handle the answer. "Is it possible to ... cut them out or something?"

Walker hesitates again, tilting her head so another lock of golden hair escapes her ear and falls onto her cheek. This time she just lets it hang there.

"The official answer is no," she says. "We haven't even been able to free any of the children from the hospitals without them going into a coma and ... passing away within a very short time. So, we haven't had a lot of chances to operate. Not on living patients, at least."

She pauses, meets Randall's gaze, and then lifts her hands up in front of her.

"But that's not necessarily the definitive answer. Because there is one kid out there who survived being disconnected from the IV rack."

"Billy," Randall says, looking down at his folded hands. "Billy survived."

"He did, Mr. Morgan. Your son survived, and we believe it's because he was disconnected from his IV before all five parasites had gotten into his blood system. I ... I also have a theory that this could be the explanation as to why ..."

"Why Billy has become their leader," David suggests. "It's all connected, isn't it?"

Walker looks over at Randall with a strange, almost guilt-ridden look. Then she nods and walks back to the light board, where she points to one of the pictures.

"Does the concept *executive functions* mean anything to you?" she asks, and when both Randall and David shake their heads, she nods. "Okay. The short version is that 'executive functions' is an umbrella term for a series of complex circuits inside the human brain. They are what enable us to solve problems in a focused manner, meaning through planning, assessing, and adapting. In other words, it is what you lack to a greater or lesser extent if you suffer from developmental disorders such as ADHD, OCD, and autism."

She picks up a marker and draws a ring around the upper part of the brain in the scan.

"Brain research hasn't yet given us a precise location for where they sit, but we do know that all of the executive functions are critically dependent on the prefrontal cortex."

Inside the previous ring, she draws another. This one encircles one of the white, drop-shaped spots. One of the creepy tadpoles.

"In the children from the hospitals, the executive functions are greatly impaired, and of the five different types of parasites, we believe that it's this one that is to blame. That it is the one that makes them act like mindless lemmings, driven only by the parasites' collective survival instincts and desire for dominance."

"But if their goal is to live forever, they would have a will, wouldn't they?" Randall interjects. "They couldn't do that if they didn't somehow ... think."

"To some extent, that's true," Walker admits. "But it's not an *individual* will."

"What do you mean?"

"The empirical evidence from our experiments with living parasites has shown—quite unequivocally—that they don't have a subjective drive but are controlled by a form of collective consciousness. A hive mind."

"What, like insects?"

Walker looks at David and nods in approval.

"Like some insects, yes," she says. "They operate

with a common goal in the same way that, for instance, ants or bees do. Furthermore, we have reason to believe that they have some kind of telepathic connection."

"Now, hold up," Randall exclaims. "Now we're getting a bit too far into science fiction territory for my taste. Are you saying that they communicate by the power of thought?"

"We *live* in a science fiction movie," David says dryly, his voice devoid of humor. "That hasn't dawned on you yet?"

"What I'm saying is that they at least are capable of receiving messages via telepathy," Walker explains. "What's interesting—and frightening—is that your son also seems to stand out from the rest in that respect because he was disconnected before getting all five parasites into his system."

She points up to the white drop, around which she has drawn a circle, in the scan.

"If I'm right, it's a parasite of exactly that type that remains in the IV bag you brought us," she says. "My theory is that Billy has retained his executive functions because the parasite that should have attached itself to his prefrontal cortex never got the chance to do so. For lack of better words, you could say that it has made him a kind of hybrid between a human and the UPPs. Someone who can communicate with the parasites and shares their intentions, but who, unlike the others, is also able to plan ahead and make conscious choices."

"So, by freeing Billy from the hospital, we made him even more dangerous?"

The realization of what it actually is that David is saying hits Randall, and he feels his throat narrowing. As if some invisible hands have closed around it, gradually squeezing.

"Keep in mind that it's just a theory for now," Walker says. "Until we've confirmed that it's the prefrontal cortex parasite that's in Billy's IV bag, we can't know anything for sure. And even if it turns out that it is, it's still only an interpretation."

Her voice has a calming tone ... but it is put-on. Randall doesn't doubt that for a second. The way she cringes and stares at him, as if she's trying to read his reaction, only confirms it. She presents it as one possible answer, but Walker is confident in her theory. She knows what her colleague is going to tell her after examining the IV bag.

"But it is the most likely explanation, isn't it?" David asks. "That Billy is able to lead them because we took him out from that hospital."

Walker takes a deep breath, holds it in for a moment, and lets it out with a sigh. Then she nods slowly, and Randall's hand—without him even registering it—reaches out and finds the edge of the desk. Latches onto it.

"It's my fault," he says in a quivering voice. "Everything that's happened. I insisted on freeing Billy, and if I hadn't, they wouldn't have been able to plan the ambush in Redwater. Then Tommy would still be alive, and—"

He stiffens and looks—through a foggy veil—over at David.

"Oh my God, David. What Billy did to Rose, I ..."

David doesn't meet his gaze. His full focus is on Helen Walker.

"There's one thing that doesn't make sense," he says. "One of the things Billy did back then was to provoke a fight between Randall and his brother, so he could have uninterrupted access to the radio out on the farm. We assumed it was to communicate with the other kids ... but that makes no sense if he could have just contacted them telepathically."

"You may well have been right in your assumption," Walker says. "We do believe that Billy is leading the children using the collective consciousness of parasites, yes. But it also seems that he can only do it within a limited radius."

"So, he has to be close to them?"

"We think so, yes. It would also explain why his flock grows larger every time they move to a new place."

"Because they're picking up strays," Randall mutters as the Oliver Twist girl with the utility knife once again flickers onto his inner cinema screen.

"Precisely," Walker says. "All of the UPP-infected children exhibit the same aggressive and murderous behavior, but Billy's flock in Pennsylvania is the only case we know of so far where they congregate and work together."

"Can you fix him?" David suddenly asks. "If we

get hold of Billy and bring him back here, can you then fix him?"

"Maybe we can do more than just that," Walker says, after which she turns toward Randall and locks her gaze on him. "Your son is special, Mr. Morgan. For better or worse. His hybrid characteristics make him dangerous, yes. But on the other hand, they may give us a deeper insight into our enemies than anything else has been able to, and ... I'm not going to lie to you. Potentially, Billy could be the key to saving all of humanity."

These are powerful words, and for a moment they are allowed to hang in the air while Randall and David stare silently at the brain scans up on the board.

They're still standing that way, undoubtedly with many of the same thoughts roaming around inside their heads, when there's a soft knock on the door and a little man in a blue lab coat sticks his head in.

"Am I interrupting, Helen?"

"It's okay, Charlie," Walker says and then points down towards the narrow, brown folder he holds in his hand. "Is that the results?"

The man replies with a nod and hands the folder over to her. She opens it, skims the papers—and nods, first to herself, then to Randall and David.

part 2

THE SAWMILL

"Drip ... drop ... drip ... drop.
Ticking away like a grandfather clock.
Time is but drops in a plastic bag."
—*O. E. Geralt,* The Book of Awesome Quotes.

chapter 7

"Are you sure you still want to do this? It's not too late to back out."

Randall looks up at David and then out at the large, open space between ARL's buildings. The weather has been a bit warmer in the last few days, so there's not as much snow as when they arrived at this place, but it's still cold enough for him to see his own breath.

"I'm sure," he says, while scratching at the wood on the armrest of the bench. "I just needed some fresh air before we start. We've been on the road too long, I think. Gotten used to it."

David lets out a strange sound that lies somewhere between a snort and a dry chuckle.

"Yeah, that's true," he says, nodding toward the

building where they've been allowed to spend the last couple of nights. "Two nights on the same mattress under the same roof, and I'm about to go crazy. But hey, if all goes well today ..."

He doesn't finish the sentence, nor does he need to. Randall knows that it's the meeting they're about to attend that David is referring to. The meeting where they find out if today is the day they leave to go after Billy.

"The wait probably doesn't help either," Randall says. "But we have to be sure."

David raises one eyebrow and squints at him.

"You're starting to sound like her. You realize that, don't you?"

"Like who? Helen?"

David nods, and Randall shrugs.

"Maybe. But she does have a point. It makes more sense to wait until we've confirmed that it's Billy's group."

"I hate to break it to you, Randall, but who else would it be? I mean, come on."

Reluctantly, but also in full recognition that David is right, Randall shrugs. The description of the size of the group of children that ARL's scouts have tracked down should in itself be enough to settle the matter. Still, both Walker and Andrews strongly insist on getting visual confirmation of the leader before setting anything in motion.

"And by the way," David says, now with a more laid-back sound in his voice and something as rare as the hint of a smile at the corner of his mouth. "When did she go from being Dr. Walker to being Helen?"

Randall doesn't answer. He just pushes himself up from the bench, then starts walking over toward the freight elevator. Part of him expects—maybe even *hopes*—that there will come another teasing comment from David, but the young man simply catches up with him and doesn't say a word until they've made it all the way down to the basement. And by then, his voice is back to its usual, life-weary tone.

"I hope they have some good news and keep it brief so we can get going soon. Otherwise, we run the risk of Billy being long gone."

"If it's true that they've stayed in that area for

weeks, they'll probably still be there tomorrow, don't you think?"

Though Randall—trying to be the grown-up and the patient opposite of David's impatience—responds this way, a part of him feels the same frustration. A part of him would like to tell Miss Senior Researcher, Biochemistry that if she just gets the operating table ready, he'll handle his part and go get Billy right away.

But he also realizes that it's not that simple. That there is too much at stake. For her, as well.

When they arrive at the meeting room, the door is already open, and they find Helen Walker in there, standing in front of a whiteboard that she is wiping clean with a cloth.

"Helen?" Randall says, ignoring the look David sends him. "Can we come in?"

"Yes, of course," she replies, making a sweeping motion toward the table in the middle. "You just take a seat wherever you want."

"And the others?"

"They're on their way. Andrews went upstairs to pick up your travel companion."

It takes a second before Randall realizes what she is saying. In fact, the penny doesn't really drop until he notices the crooked smile on her lips and rewinds the sentence in his head.

"So, it's happening?"

Walker nods.

"We got visual confirmation. One of our scouts spotted a boy yesterday who fits Billy's description and who clearly has a leading role. The scout has been following him and gave us the confirmation this morning."

"Was Billy ... did he look okay?"

Even though she is trying to hide it, Randall sees Walker making a strained swallowing motion, and he immediately regrets asking the question.

But it's too late. The answer is coming.

"He organized an assault on a camp of about fifty people in Multon, none of whom survived," she says, looking down at the floor. "So yes, I'd say he seems to be up and about."

"When ... um, when are we scheduled to leave then?" David asks.

Walker looks at him, opens her mouth, but then

closes it again and turns to Randall.

"That wasn't nice," she says. "I'm still a bit shocked from finding out myself, and then it just flew out of me, I guess. I'd like to apologize for that."

"It's okay," Randall replies, trying to mean it sincerely. "I know he's not the same anymore."

Walker nods, David nods, and then the room is filled with a suffocating, awkward silence that neither of them is able to break. Therefore, it is a relief when two short knocks sound on the doorframe shortly after.

"We're here," says Captain Andrews.

Andrews is the man who accompanied Walker in the room that the guards initially put Randall and David in. Since then, they've found out that he's the highest-ranking leader at ARL—even if he's still just wearing a woolen sweater and a pair of jeans.

Behind Andrews is another man whom Randall also recognizes, though he hasn't got the faintest idea what his name is. It is one of the two soldiers who blinded them with a flash grenade and then locked them up.

At least it's the nice one, he thinks. *It could have been his trigger-happy partner.*

"This is Ollie Moses," Andrews says, nodding toward the soldier. "He's joining you."

Moses greets them with a nod and a smile, whereafter he walks over to the table, pulls out a chair, and takes a seat. So does Andrews.

"Everyone here knows what's at stake," Walker begins. "So, I don't want to waste time repeating that. Instead, I will give a brief summary of your task, so everyone is on the same page."

She turns around and starts writing on the whiteboard.

BILLY MORGAN.

COLMENA.

SCOTT WILEY.

TINFIELDS SAWMILL.

"As you know, it's Billy Morgan, Randall's son, who is our primary objective, and we've got visual confirmation today that he's in the area around Colmena with a group of UPP-infected children he appears to be leading."

"How big a flock are we talking about?" Moses asks.

Walker shrugs and, with a glance, passes the question on to Captain Andrews.

"I don't have the exact number," he says. "But expect it to be high. We've had three scouts on them for a while and they say the flock is constantly growing. That they follow a fixed pattern of staying in an area for a period of time, emptying it of food and exterminating survivor camps, while recruiting more of their ... child soldiers. They say they pull them in like magnets."

Randall feels David's gaze drift over to him, and when he meets it, he instinctively knows that they're both thinking back on the same words.

A collective consciousness, like some insects.

Telepathy.

"But even though Billy Morgan is the main objective, your first task is to meet up with Scott Wiley at the sawmill in Tinfields," Walker continues. "He's the scout group's leader. They know the routines of the flock, and they will help you plan—and afterwards complete—the mission."

"How long is the trip over there?" David asks.

"Since both Tinfields and Colmena are located in southwestern Pennsylvania, you'll probably need to stop somewhere along the way to spend the night. But there's a vehicle being prepped for you right now, and if you leave soon, you should be able to reach Tinfields by tomorrow afternoon."

"I'd like to go back to the size of the flock for a moment," Moses says, and when Walker nods, he turns his gaze over to Captain Andrews. "It sounds like we're talking about an actual *army* of—pardon my French—brainwashed child soldiers. And my math says three from here plus three scouts. That makes six in total. Six men ... against a flock that has exterminated one camp of survivors after another on their trip down through Pennsylvania."

"I hear what you're saying," Andrews replies. "And if the purpose was a confrontation, we obviously wouldn't send such a small group off alone. But the purpose isn't to seek out a conflict. The objective is to get a hold of Billy Morgan. Preferably without anyone even noticing."

"And them?" Moses asks, gesturing at Randall

and David. "With all due respect, it's a pretty delicate mission, and you're not exactly trained professionals."

"Hey, we've been living out there for over two years," David replies promptly—and in a voice that doesn't hide his outrage.

Moses holds his hands disarmingly up in front of him, as if to say: *I didn't mean to offend you, kid.* However, he doesn't have time to actually say the words before Walker breaks in.

"Randall and David have several things to offer regarding this mission," she says. "They were both present during the Redwater massacre and they know Billy Morgan better than anyone. The mere fact that Randall is his father could prove to be an advantage if ..."

If there's anything human left inside Billy, Randall has time to think, but what Walker actually ends the sentence with is:

"... if it can make the kids hesitate."

She pauses, standing with her hands on her hips, staring at Moses the way a carpenter looks at a piece of furniture he has just assembled.

"Besides, I think you'd have a hard time finding anyone more motivated than these two," she says.

Moses looks back and forth between Randall and David, both of whom meet his gaze and don't shy away from it. Then he leans back in his chair and shows his acceptance by blinking his eyes once and nodding.

"How do we get in contact with the scouts?"

"There's a radio in the truck," Andrews says. "It's preset to the frequency Wiley's team uses, and they'll be expecting to hear from you at noon tomorrow. By then, you should be well within range of them."

After those words, Andrews looks back and forth between Randall, David, and Ollie Moses—and when none of them says anything, he lets his gaze drift up to Helen Walker.

"Well, I suppose that's it," she says, shrugging. "How about we get you guys on the road then?"

chapter 8

"Oh, piss off."

"I'm not kidding. It *is* me, I swear."

Ollie Moses—whom Randall must admit he's starting to grow fond of—shifts his gaze from the road ahead for a moment to stare at him with small, skeptical eyes.

"*The Flood, Traveler's Guilt, The Lost Man*. You expect me to believe you're *that* Randall Morgan?"

Randall nods and points his thumb toward the back of the truck.

"Ask David when he wakes up."

"Didn't you say that you guys met *after* the Collapse?" Ollie asks. "Then he wouldn't know for sure either, would he?"

"Fair point," Randall admits. "But they're still my

books."

Ollie looks at him again, and this time the suspicion is replaced with recognition. Maybe even admiration.

Oh, Mr. Morgan, I'm just your biggest fan, Allie taunts in the back of Randall's head. *Does it feel good to get your ego polished up a bit, Randall? Nice to think about something other than the mass murderous son you failed?*

Actually, it *is* nice. He's not even ashamed to admit it. It allows him to believe, if but for a fleeting instant, that this version of Randall Morgan, the author, didn't pass away along with all the others during the Collapse.

Moreover, his inner version of his ex-wife will have to do better if she intends to hurt him with her snide comments. Because there hasn't been—and never will be—a single day since Redwater that Randall isn't haunted by bad conscience and doubt. Where the question of whether he could have stopped Billy doesn't rumble in the back of his mind.

"*The Flood* was the best, if you ask me," Ollie says.

"The twist at the end, where their son turns out to be the villain, it was just so ..."

He realizes the cruel irony of fate and stops mid-sentence as his face struggles to find a suitable grimace.

"It's okay," Randall says. "I've made that parallel myself before, believe me."

"Yeah, I suppose you have," Ollie replies softly, and after that he doesn't say anything for quite a while.

Neither does Randall. He just sits in silence, watching the world outside the window as it whizzes by.

Right now, though, there aren't many interesting things to spot, as they're driving on a main road that cuts through a rather flat and unvarying countryside ... which moreover is covered with a thin layer of snow, so there is not even a little color variation.

The interior of their vehicle isn't exactly mind-blowing either. In here, it's dark green instead of snowy white that dominates, but the degree of variation is roughly the same. The most intriguing sight is the dancing spring puppet mounted on the dashboard—Neo from *The Matrix* in the famous bent-over-backwards pose, so it looks like he's dodging bullets in slow motion every time the truck hits a bump.

The puppet is pretty funny in Randall's opinion, especially considering that someone decided to place it on the dashboard of a military vehicle. Nevertheless, its novelty wore off after the first twenty minutes on the road. Since then, nearly five hours have passed.

"We've got at least an hour's drive to go before we get to Merryway, where we're going to spend the night," Ollie says, as Randall raises his hand in front of his mouth and yawns. "So, if you need to rest your eyelids a bit, feel free. I'll be sure to wake you up if they release a trailer for a new Marvel movie or something like that."

The comment makes Randall chuckle and shake his head.

"Yeah, that would be something. But no thanks, I'm not that tired, so I think I'll wait."

"Up to you," Ollie says, moving his gaze back to

the road ahead.

Meanwhile, Randall leans to the side and puts his elbow up on the edge under the window so he can rest his head on his arm. And as he sits there, listening to the crunching sound of snow being flattened under the tires, his eyelids do start to feel heavy after all.

He blinks, blinks again, and suddenly he is no longer in the passenger seat of a military truck. He's outside, on a large playground, staring at an empty swing while a whirlwind of icy snowflakes dances rapidly around him.

The rest of the playground is also empty, just like the swings, yet it's as though he can hear ... life? As if a distant echo of the children who once played here still hangs in the air.

Behind the playground is a building whose function and purpose are revealed with what can be seen through its windows: large whiteboards, alphabet posters, rows of chairs and tables.

A freezing sensation hits the back of his neck as he sees the words written—not with a marker pen, but with screaming yellow spray paint—across one of the boards.

DON'T CALL THE POLICE! THEY'RE THE ONES KILLING PEOPLE!

A sound—the loud, piercing howl of a police siren—makes him stiffen ... but when he turns around, there is nothing. No patrol cars and no homicidal officers. Only a deserted and empty street out on the other side of the playground's enclosure. A street that—as an almost sarcastic underlining of how empty it is—has a sign with the name *TUMBLEWEED CROSSING*.

Confused and a little shaken, he slowly turns back toward the playground—and stiffens once more.

The swing isn't empty anymore. There's a kid sitting on it. A boy. He's sitting with his back turned, so Randall can't see his face, but the bright hair and the body posture could well look like ...

With a creeping sense that the ground beneath his feet is as fragile as the surface of a forest lake, where winter's first fledgling layer of ice has only just formed, Randall takes a step closer. Then another.

The chains on the swing rattle as the boy jumps off without warning.

For a moment he remains standing where he landed. Then he glances back over his shoulder, winks at his father with one eye, and starts running towards the school building.

Soaked in panic, Randall follows. He runs, trips on the icy tiles, falls, gets back up, and continues as his son's puffer coat fades behind the double glass doors of the school entrance.

He reaches out, grabs the handle of the doors, and pulls.

"Billy? Billy, wait for me!"

The long, semi-dark hallway behind the doors grabs the words, rips them apart, and throws them back at him in small fragments.

He runs forward, listening for something, *anything*, that can tell him where his son has gone. On both sides of him, doors and bulletin boards glide by.

Now there is something. Two sounds: a heavy scraping, as if someone were dragging a piece of heavy furniture across a tile floor, and a brief, shrill burst of laughter of the type one only hears in schoolyards or behind the barred windows of an asylum for the mentally ill.

Randall follows the sounds. They lead him down a side aisle where someone, for whatever reason, has left an empty bed in the middle of the floor. One of the kinds with wheels that are used in hospitals, mind you.

After edging past the bed, he follows the sounds once again—and he realizes that what sounded like laughter before is really something else. It's the sound of frustration and exertion. The sound of a child trying to lift something that's too heavy.

As soon as he turns the corner and sees the sign, Randall instinctively knows it's in there that the sound originates from.

SCHOOL LIBRARY

ELLIE-MAY KAUFMANN ELEMENTARY

He opens the door and enters a library that is far too big, far too old-fashioned, and far too imposing to belong to this school. It looks like something taken out of a castle in the Middle Ages.

The smell alone—a mixture of dust and old

paper—gives him the feeling of having stepped through a portal to another world.

Now he catches sight of him. Billy. His little bumblebee.

The boy is once again standing with his back to him, and he doesn't appear to have registered his father's presence. His attention is turned toward the door whose handle he is grasping with both hands.

It's the door to the library's *ARCHIVE*. At least that's what it says on the sign that hangs on the wall to the left of the door—a bit above the spot where Billy has placed his foot to push off from the wall while he tries to pull the door open.

"Billy?" Randall says, but the shock and confusion have pulled all the strength out of his voice, and the sound isn't loud enough to drown out the boy's moans and hisses as he struggles with the door.

"Billy?" he repeats, a little louder. "What are you doing?"

For a moment, the boy freezes in the middle of the motion, and the sound of rattling hinges stops.

Then he sighs in despair.

"I ... can't ... get ... the door ... open, Dad."

"What's in there?"

No response.

"Do you want me to help you?"

The boy looks at him with a pair of eyes that could melt hearts and topple fortresses.

"Would you?"

"Of course, honey," Randall says, and when the boy steps aside, he grabs the doorknob. "Let's see if I can get it open."

He pulls—and is on the verge of tumbling over backwards as the door effortlessly and without a sound flips open.

"Thanks, Dad," Billy says, pushing past him into the room, where he steers straight over to a dusty bookcase. From it he pulls down a cardboard box, filled to the brim with loose sheets of paper.

"Billy, wait," Randall says. "There's so much I'd like to—"

"Not now, Dad. I need to find this. Later, okay?"

"But I ..." Randall starts, but the look he receives from the boy makes him change his mind. "Alright,

Billy. Later."

The boy doesn't answer. He's far too preoccupied with pulling up papers, skimming them, and
then tossing them aside.

This goes on for a while—him pulling up papers,
reading, and throwing them away in frustration.
But then, suddenly, there's a sheet that makes him
hesitate.

He reads it, narrows his eyes, reads it again—
and then smiles broadly.

"Finally."

"What is it?" Randall asks, taking a step forward.
"What did you find?"

Billy looks up at him and then hurries to fold up
the paper ... but there are only four words on it, and
Randall has time to read them.

SCOTT WILEY. TINFIELDS. SAWMILL.

He opens his mouth to ask what on earth Billy is
planning to do with that paper, but before he has a
chance to say anything, the boy leaps forward and
pushes him in the chest, tipping him over backwards, not just out through the doorway, but *downward*. Into a deep hole, where he falls and falls, until

he opens his eyes with a jolt and sees his own pale, terrified face in the side window of the military truck.

"Are you okay?" he hears David ask from the back. "It sounded pretty bad."

Randall blinks a few times and then looks over at Ollie Moses, who is still sitting behind the wheel.

"The kid is right. It didn't sound too pleasant."

"I'm okay," Randall replies, and after a moment's hesitation, he adds, mostly to convince himself: "It was just a dream."

chapter 9

An hour and a half later, Randall, David, and Ollie are sitting in a semicircle around an open fireplace, staring into the flames. Around them, shadows dance on the walls, making the living room of this ordinary townhouse in Merryway look like a witch's hut from a Grimm fairy tale.

Once, this house belonged to Ollie's uncle, and though it was something he only briefly mentioned when they arrived, it's clear that it was someone he'd spent a lot of time with. The first evidence of this was that he instinctively knew where everything was—kindling for the fireplace, a lighter and some old newspapers to get it going. The second piece of evidence was the sad and thoughtful expression his eyes have had ever since they came in through the door.

Outside, the world has turned dark. When looking out the large patio door only a faint outline of the hedge around the garden of the house can be glimpsed.

"How's the food coming?" David asks.

Ollie shrugs, then grabs a tool from the rack next to the fireplace—a long pincer, resembling those used to flip hot dogs on a barbeque grill. With it, he gently lifts one of the two cans out of the fire and looks down into it.

"Five more minutes," he says, and David replies with a half-hearted *thank you*, which most of all sounds like a dying man's last, rasping breath, after which he gets up.

"Where are you going?"

"I might as well empty my bladder while we wait for the food."

"Be careful," Randall says, halfway expecting it to trigger a sulky answer. But David merely nods and then disappears out of the room.

"It hasn't been easy for him, has it?" Ollie says, when David is completely out of sight.

Randall shakes his head.

"It hasn't, no. David has been plagued by a special kind of bad luck."

"Meaning what?"

"Meaning that he has had everything taken away from him ... twice. He lost his family and friends during the Collapse, like most, but for David it didn't stop there."

He hesitates for a moment, and as he does so, something silvery appears at the edge of his field of vision. A pocket flask.

He looks over at Ollie, then nods and takes the little metal bottle.

The booze is lukewarm, and the only taste he is able to identify is metal. However, the after-effect—the burning sensation in his throat and stomach—still remains.

"We managed to build a life for ourselves," he continues. "Against all odds, we somehow made things work. We lived on my brother's farm, traded with other survivors—and in one of their camps, David even found a girlfriend. Rose. That was her name. Actually, they, um ... they had just moved in together when ..."

"When Redwater happened?" Ollie asks, and when Randall nods, he offers him the pocket flask once more. Randall accepts it.

"Rose was the first one Billy killed," he says. "He pushed her off a platform. She fell down onto a concrete staircase. Broke her neck."

"Shit."

"Yeah, shit," Randall says, and for a moment— perhaps because this mysterious, shadowy living room invites the sharing of secrets—he's tempted to put into words the one burden he can't share with David. Tempted to open up about the suspicion he had but never got confirmed by Rose. Tempted to reveal that he thinks David's loss on that fateful day in Redwater might have been greater than the young man himself realized, and that Rose's life might not have been the only one that ended in the collision with that concrete staircase.

In the end, though, he chooses to keep it to himself. Perhaps because he is afraid that by saying it out loud, he would somehow make it real.

"What about you?" he asks instead, handing the bottle back to Ollie. "What's yours?"

"My what?"

"Your tragedy," Randall says, giving him a faint smile. "If the Collapse has taught me anything, it's that everyone has a sad story. So, what's yours?"

Ollie ponders for a moment, twisting and turning the little metal flask in his hands.

"At best, it's going to make me sound like a weirdo," he says. "At worst, like a real jerk. Just keep in mind that it was you who wanted to know, okay? You asked me."

"Well, you've definitely piqued my curiosity."

Ollie smiles and shrugs slightly.

"I lived a modest life. No wife, no children ... and the only family I had left was Steven, my uncle."

"The guy who owned this house, right?"

"Yep," Ollie replies as he pulls a loose thread out of the stitching on his pants, rolls it up into a small ball, and flicks it into the fireplace. "That was him. He's gone now, but he was already living on borrowed time back then, lung cancer, so when it all went to hell, he pulled a Kurt Cobain and clocked out. So, the biggest loss I suffered was ... well, Miss Furbelly. My cat."

"Miss Furbelly?" Randall repeats, raising one eyebrow.

"I told you it would make me sound like a jerk."

"Not a jerk," Randall replies dryly. "Just a weirdo."

Ollie chuckles, then lifts up the pocket flask and gives it a flick forward in the air as if clinking an invisible glass.

"Who's a weirdo?" David asks from the doorway behind them. "Walker?"

"You better watch it, kid," Ollie says, but he doesn't sound angry. "That's my colleague you're talking about."

"That may be," David says as he walks over and takes a seat next to them. "But there's something about her. She's pretty ... intense."

"That she is," Ollie admits. "I don't know if we'll ever beat those damned parasites, but if I had to put my money on someone to do it, I'd bet it all on Helen Walker. She's tough as an old boot, that woman."

"Has she always been like that?"

For a moment, Randall's question causes Ollie's face to contract, making two deep, furrowed wrinkles appear on the skin of his forehead. Then he shakes his head.

"Not in the same way. She was tough before, but it was more of a facade, I think. The way women had to act if they wanted to survive in a workplace where 95 percent of the colleagues were men. Now she *is* tough, and I don't think there's a lot of thoughts left in her head that aren't about those fucking parasites."

Before continuing, Ollie leans forward and glances into the cans inside the fireplace, then grabs the barbeque pincer again and fishes them both out.

"Of course, I realize it's only natural for her to want to understand them, being a biochemist and all," he continues, after all three of them have gotten a bowlful of chili con carne. "But it's more than just that. She's *obsessed* with them. Obsessed with the idea of having them exterminated."

"But that's only positive, right?" Randall asks. "I

mean, who wouldn't like to see them eradicated and the children saved? And if she actually has the skills to do either, then ..."

Ollie looks at him, and for a split second there's something in his eyes that Randall can't decipher. Something that at the same time feels both important and intimidating. Before he can react to it, though, it's gone, and Ollie smiles avertedly.

"You're right, of course," he says. "Don't listen to me, I'm talking nonsense. I'm hungry and tired, that's all."

"So, you've been living at the research center all this time?" David asks.

"More or less. Given that the place had a security bunker with its own generator and enough food for a small country, it was sort of the obvious choice for most people to just stay there. Of course, there were those who chose to risk their lives to get home. Those who had families, you know, but ... well, let's just say I doubt it went well for most of them."

He pauses as he eats a spoonful of chili con carne and stares blankly into the flames.

"I'll never forget the first time I ventured out," he

says. "It must have been after a few months. It was ... I mean, we had it described to us, but to see it in real life, to *see* people hanging from lampposts like that—it was terrifying."

Randall nods, and for a split second, Ollie's story has pushed him out of time and space. For a split second, it has brought him back to the driver's seat of his old car, where he sits with his hands glued to the steering wheel, staring at the hanged man out on the other side of the rain-soaked windshield. His first encounter with the macabre street art of the police force.

He jolts as something touches his arm. It's David, holding up one of the cans and nodding toward Randall's bowl to ask if he wants another portion.

"No, thank you, David," Randall replies, shaking his head. "I'm not really that hungry."

"What about you guys?" Ollie asks. "After what happened in Redwater, I mean. That can't have been an easy time either."

Which part of it? Allie scoffs in the back of Randall's head. *That our son killed hundreds of people in cold blood, or that David saw his girlfriend being tossed down onto a concrete staircase? You have to ask him to be a little more specific.*

"It wasn't," David says in a voice that makes him sound twenty years older.

"We were both in a very dark place," Randall adds. "Everyone we knew and everything we had was gone, and we had no choice but to run with our tails between our legs. We went from having two homes—my brother's farm and the camp in San Hiva—to living a life on the road with no home at all because nowhere felt safe anymore. It was as if, overnight, we had gotten thrown back to day one. Like the way it was back in the beginning of the Collapse, when you didn't know if you could trust anyone."

"Except it wasn't police officers we were afraid to see when we looked back over our shoulders," David adds. "It was kids."

Randall nods and hears himself utter a dry, joyless chuckle.

"You'd think we'd have gotten tougher after the first time, but ... if we hadn't had each other, I'm not sure we would have made it."

"But you did."

"Barely, yes."

"And then what changed?"

"What do you mean?"

"You came to us," Ollie elaborates. "That must have required quite a bit of blind faith, right?"

"We found the IV bag," Randall says. "And it wasn't empty. That's what changed. As soon as I saw that little vermin floating around in there, I knew we had to get it to you guys. To Helen."

That's not the whole truth. What Randall fails to mention is that Newcrest Memorial wasn't the first hospital he visited in the post-Redwater period. That he had been to many other hospitals hoping to find something similar, each and every time walking away empty-handed.

Nor does he mention that he only returned to the hospital in Newcrest because he eventually saw no other options—and that deep down he had decided that it would be his final stop if the bag under Billy's seat wasn't there.

"Then we'll just have to pray that Helen is right in all her theories," Ollie says while getting up and gathering the empty bowls in a stack. Next, he places the two cans on top of them. "And now I suggest you pick out a couple of good sleeping spots for the night. In the meantime, I'll heat a pot of snow and do the dishes."

"You want a hand?"

"Three bowls and three spoons," Ollie says, looking down at the stack in his hands. "I think I'll manage. It's more important that you get a good night's sleep."

Randall consents with a thumbs-up and then turns his attention to David, who immediately nods. Then David gets up and walks over to their bags, where he pulls out pads and sleeping bags and throws them over to Randall, who rolls them out on the floor.

After such a long time together on the road, it's a well-rehearsed process, and in a matter of seconds, both their beds are ready.

Unfortunately, Randall knows from experience that the ensuing ritual—the struggle to fall asleep—rarely is completed that fast.

chapter 10

Crackling, popping, and crunching. That's all. No voices, no response. No Scott Wiley.

"I don't get it," Ollie sighs for what must be the sixth or seventh time. "They're *scouts*. Punctuality should be their top priority."

He moves to hang the radio transmitter back in place, but then hesitates and lifts it up in front of his mouth one more time.

"Calling Scott Wiley. This is Corporal Ollie Moses of ARL, Maryland. Come in, Wiley. Come in, somebody ... oh, fuck it!"

He moves the transmitter away from his mouth again and this time puts it back in its holder.

"What now?" David asks from the back.

Ollie doesn't answer right away. He sits with

both hands—slightly quivering—clenched around the steering wheel. Then he pushes his lower lip forward and breathes out some air.

"Tinfields is still our best bet," he says. "We know the scouts have been camped at the sawmill there, so we have to at least check it out."

Something about that strategy bothers Randall, but since he can't quite put his finger on why, he keeps it to himself.

"How far are we from Tinfields?" he asks instead.

"An hour, more or less," Ollie says as he puts the truck in gear and starts driving. "And if I have a say in it, it's going to be the latter. I honestly don't like this."

"You're not the only one," Randall says. "What do we do if they're not there anymore?"

"We'll cross that bridge if and when we get to it. For now, we'll just have to cross our fingers and hope that it's a technical glitch. That their power generator is down or something like that so they're unable to receive our transmissions."

Part of Randall is annoyed at Ollie for shying

away from the question, but once more he chooses to let it go. Besides, he already knows the answer. Because without the help of the military scouts, the task of finding Billy in Colmena is comparable to looking for a polar bear in a blizzard or a black cat in a coal mine.

It's not a very encouraging thought, so he decides to push it aside and cling to Ollie's logic—that it's a problem they'll deal with *if* and *when* it arises.

It's an excellent strategy, and it works for him, too—at least until, a little under an hour later, they get their first glimpse of the sawmill in Tinfields.

Or rather; what they assume is the sawmill in Tinfields, since all they can actually see is a large, thick column of smoke that stands like a dark tower in front of the gray sky ahead.

"What the hell?" Ollie murmurs, upon which he—maybe consciously, maybe unconsciously—steps harder on the accelerator.

"Is it burning?" David asks.

"Looks like it," Randall says. "But we don't know for sure if it's—"

"It's the sawmill, alright," Ollie says, pointing to

a spot to the right of the building where the smoke originates. "Do you see the brown thingy on the hill over there, the one that looks like a roller coaster? It's a chute that you use to transport the lumber from the road directly down to the saws."

Randall follows the direction of his finger and realizes that their driver is right, unfortunately.

"David, the guns are in my bag, would you—"

"On it," David replies, and a few seconds later his hand appears on the left side of Randall's shoulder. In it is his Smith & Wesson.

Randall takes the gun, checks that it's loaded, and puts it in the pocket of his jacket. Then he rolls the window down a little on his side, hoping that a bit of air will soothe his nerves and clear his head.

It works, but only to a certain extent. For although the air is cool, it carries with it a heavy, coal-like smell that burns in his throat.

As they approach the sawmill, Ollie slows down gradually, and by the time they turn into the large, graveled space in front of the burning building, he doesn't even touch the gas pedal anymore. He simply lets the truck roll until it stops on its own, while he himself sits paralyzed, staring out the windshield.

But when Randall grabs the door handle, wanting to open the door, the paralysis suddenly breaks and Ollie grabs his arm.

"Hold up," he says. "This wasn't an accident."

"What do you mean?"

Ollie points down to the ground in front of the building, where an object lies in the gravel. At first, Randall has a hard time figuring out what it is, because it's located at an angle where it catches and reflects the orange-red flames behind the windows of the sawmill's main building. To him it mostly looks like a small pool of liquid fire in the middle of the gravel.

Then he simultaneously realizes what it is and what Ollie meant.

The object is a broken bottle, and it doesn't take much imagination to envision that it probably contained a highly flammable liquid, and that this is the cause of the large, scorched stain on the wall above it.

In the wake of that realization, another follows.

This smashed bottle is far from the only one. When Randall lets his gaze slide around—first up on the building and then across the gravel—he sees several dark spots on the facade and plenty of glass shards on the ground.

Molotov cocktails. Someone has carpet-bombed the sawmill with Molotov cocktails.

Hardly has he finished this deduction before something hits the windshield and turns it into a vivid painting of flames in blue and orange colors.

"IT'S AN AMBUSH!" Ollie roars through the whistling snake hiss of the fire. "WE NEED TO GET OUT OF HERE!"

Randall hears him, but for a moment he's unable to do anything but sit and stare at the windshield while one single thought, stubbornly as a mantra, runs in circles in his head.

Not again. Not again. Not again.

Only when he hears another bottle hit the truck is he able to break free from the shock and move. Because this time it's somewhere in the back—and David doesn't have a windshield or metal doors to protect him. He sits on the bed of the truck with a plastic tarp as his only shield against this rain of fire.

"DAVID? ARE YOU OKAY?"

"YES, I'M OKAY, BUT ... IT'S FUCKING *BURNING* BACK HERE."

"GRAB A HOLD OF SOMETHING, KID," Ollie yells. "I'LL DRIVE OVER TO THE PATIO ROOF OVER THERE, AND AS SOON AS WE'RE UNDER IT, YOU JUMP OUT. GOT IT?"

"GOT IT!"

Satisfied with the answer, Ollie turns his gaze back to the lower left corner of the windshield, which is the only place where he is still able to look out.

Then he steps on the pedal.

chapter 11

The patio roof under which Ollie is trying to give them shelter from the rain of fire is an elongated extension on the left side of the sawmill. As in the main building, the primary building material in this section is wood, but amazingly, the flames have not yet taken hold over there—neither in the thick posts that hold up the roof, nor in the many logs that lie in stacks below it.

It is an encounter with one of these stacks that brings the truck to such an abrupt halt that Randall only barely dodges a head-on collision with the dashboard.

"Sorry," he hears Ollie say beside him. "I couldn't see it before it was too late."

Randall makes a dismissive *forget it* motion with

his hand, then turns around in the seat so he can look at David through the hole into the bed of the truck.

"How are you doing back there?"

David lifts his thumb, but only for a brief second, before instead moving his hand over to his mouth and coughing badly. Not that there's anything surprising about that, given that the plastic cover on one side has started to curl up, giving off a thick, blueish-gray smoke.

Without hesitation—and without even considering that there may well be more Molotov cocktails heading their way—Randall pushes the door open on his side and edges out. Then he begins to pull open the metal buckles holding the tarp. It's difficult, though, as they're locked hard, and his fingers are trembling.

"David, can you hear me?"

"Yeah."

"This is going way too slow. Do you still have your knife on you?"

No answer—but a moment later, the knife blade breaks through the plastic cover and moves downwards, leaving a rift of about four feet.

Behind Randall, Ollie appears. His face is contorted and stern.

"I saw a couple of those piss-ants," he says, pointing over to a cluster of trees behind the sawmill. "They're running around over there. Little fucking gnomes."

Randall looks down at his gun and then holds it out toward him.

"Take this and cover us while I help David get out."

Ollie doesn't hesitate to take the gun, nor does he hesitate to point it at the trees and pull the trigger.

Meanwhile, Randall turns around and helps David, who is now halfway through the crack in the tarp.

When the young man is safely down from the back of the truck, Randall turns to look around.

There are no apparent escape routes and no hiding places. Their best bet is in between two large stacks of logs further over toward the main building, but seeking shelter there comes with a risk.

One well-placed Molotov cocktail, and those two stacks would go from being an impromptu trench to a death trap.

As an uncomfortable extension of this thought, there is a clank of breaking glass, followed by another snake hiss, this time from the canopy above them. A second after, droplets and thin jets of burning liquid start to fall from the edge of the roof and down between the joints of its tiles.

"Fuck this shit!" Ollie yells, firing another shot at the trees. "Die, damnit! Die, you little fuckers!"

"Over here," Randall says, pulling David with him in the direction of the two log stacks.

Once over there, they both drop to their knees and turn around so they're sitting with their backs leaned against one of the stacks.

"How many are there?" David asks, as Ollie joins them.

"Three or four. Two over by the trees and one or two out by the road where we came in."

"Two," Randall says, pointing over to the military truck, now shrouded in a column of dark, gray smoke.

"What?"

"There must have been two of them out by the road," he elaborates. "Otherwise, they couldn't possibly have hit the truck on both sides like that."

Ollie nods and then looks at David.

"How good are you with your gun, kid?"

"Good enough."

As if wanting to make sure that David's response isn't just an expression of the sometimes disastrous confidence of young men, Ollie looks at Randall.

"He *is* good," Randall says. "Better than me."

"Fine. Then you take the side facing the road, kid, and in the meantime, I'll take care of the two bastards behind the trees. I saw where they were hiding."

David nods, then he gets up on his knees and leans to the side so he can peer out past the end of the log stack.

"Do you see them?"

"There's too much smoke. I can't ... no, wait. I think there's one over there."

He raises the gun and takes aim, but is immediately stopped by Ollie, who puts his hand on his shoulder.

"Get a lock on him, but don't shoot until I say so. That way we might be able to get two of them."

For a moment, Randall doesn't understand what Ollie means. But when he sees him take his place—and then aim—over at the logs on the other side, the pieces fall into place.

"Ready, kid?" Ollie asks.

"Oh, yeah."

"Good. Then we pull the trigger in three ... two ... one ..."

The bangs from the guns hurt Randall's ears, but it's nothing compared to the sounds that follow the second after.

Because you can tell yourself they're monsters. That they are cold-blooded killers and that they are no longer human. But that doesn't change the fact that they scream with the vocal cords of a child.

"I ... I got one of them," Ollie says in a voice that reveals that their screams also affect him.

David, on the other hand, is ice-cold, both in his eyes and in his voice, as he glances over at Ollie's side and says:

"Well done. So did I. Then we just need to get the last two."

This cynical and unaffected behavior on David's part—exactly as was the case with the girl in Hollowfolk—disgusts Randall, and for a moment he feels a strong urge to rip the gun out of David's hands and scold him.

However, he hasn't got time for that, nor anything else, as a new sound now catches his attention.

Steps. Hurried steps. Someone running out on the gravel.

He pulls himself up and glances out over the edge of the stack on the right side.

Sure enough, there is one of them out there. A girl, hardly more than ten years old, with freckles on her cheeks and two bright pigtails, so tangled that they look like dreadlocks.

She's dressed in a worn-out school uniform—dark blue skirt, white polo, and a blazer—but she hasn't got a school bag. Instead, she has a bottle in her hand. A bottle that has a piece of burning cloth hanging out of its neck, making it look like a bizarre version of an Olympic torch.

With increasing terror, he watches her lift the bottle triumphantly above her head, preparing to throw.

And he *knows* she won't miss. Every cell in his body tells him that the distance between them is so short that she simply can't miss. That in a few seconds, the bottle will hit the bullseye and soak them in liquid fire. That they'll be burned alive, while—

No further does he get before the bang sounds. A devastating bang, right next to him. In its wake follows a sight that will haunt him for the rest of his days.

The bottle explodes in the girl's hand, sending a cascade of burning liquid all over her. Fluid fire that sets her pigtails, her school jacket, her polo, and finally her skirt on fire.

And she screams, but—and this is in many ways the worst part—it doesn't sound like it's in pain or panic. It sounds to be in anger and frustration.

"End it," Randall orders as the girl staggers sideways, frantically pounding away at her chest trying to put out the fire. "For God's sake, David. End it!"

David says nothing, simply raises the gun, takes aim, and plants a bullet in the dead center of the girl's forehead.

He could have done that before, too, Allie whispers in the back of Randall's head. *You know he could have, right? He didn't have to aim at the bottle.*

Randall ignores her—in part because he can't afford to shift his focus away from their bad situation yet, and in part because the thought feels like the lid of a Pandora's box.

"Oh, hell no, you don't," he hears behind him, and as he turns around, he sees Ollie leaping out from his cover and dashing off with his gun pointed toward the trees. "You stay here, you little shit!"

His prey—a boy about the same age as the girl with the pigtails—doesn't answer, but just continues to zigzag his way over toward the hill with the big lumber slide they saw when they arrived.

Two bullets he manages to dodge, but the third lands midway between his shoulder blades, putting a sudden end to his escape.

His fall is undramatic and almost completely silent. No waving his arms and no cries of pain. He just sinks to his knees for a moment, then tilts forward and lands face down on the ground.

"Was that the last of them?" David asks when Ollie comes back.

"I think so ... but it might be a good idea to go for a walk around the house to make sure."

Randall and David both nod, but nonetheless, neither of them moves from the spot before Ollie knocks the gun's muzzle against the edge of the log stack, sending them a questioning look.

"You coming?"

"Huh? Oh, yeah, sure."

chapter 12

When they stop on the other side of the sawmill's main building, Randall, David, and Ollie haven't seen any more murderous children. They have, however, located the military scouts. All three of them.

"God damnit. They didn't stand a chance."

Randall looks at Ollie and opens his mouth, but he can't think of anything relevant to say, so he closes it again and lets his gaze fall back on Scott Wiley.

Not that one would be able to determine that the charred corpse behind the metal bars actually *is* Scott Wiley, if it weren't for the chain with the dog tag around his neck.

Of the three dead scouts, Wiley is the only one

standing upright—though Randall suspects it's Wiley's head and hands holding him up rather than his feet. Because his head looks stuck between the metal bars of the window, and the hands seem to have somehow... *fused* with them.

The other two are on the floor behind him. One is charred like Wiley and looks most of all like a blend between a scaly crocodile and a naked human being. The other had managed to avoid being burned alive but was probably just suffocated by smoke instead. It definitely looks as though he was grabbing his own neck at the moment of death.

"How did they know?" David asks.

"What do you mean?"

"The kids. How the heck did they know where to find them?"

"They must have discovered that they were being watched," Ollie says, shrugging resignedly. "And then followed them here."

It's a fine theory, Allie whispers in Randall's inner ear. *Unfortunately, the two of us know that's not the right explanation.*

He knows she's right, and he also knows what he

ought to do now. That it is time to admit—to him- self as well as to his companions—that he has once again been outsmarted by his son.

But knowing doesn't make it easier. It doesn't remove the nausea that the guilt provokes, and it doesn't loosen the knot in his windpipe.

"It was Billy," he sighs. "Billy told them."

"I'm not sure I follow you," Ollie says. "Your *son* told them?"

Randall nods, and Ollie's eyes transform into two narrow lines.

"Um, okay. But ... that doesn't really answer the question, does it? Because how would your son know, then?"

"He ... um."

For a moment, Randall is unable to find fitting words for the rest of the sentence, and he hesitantly lifts a finger and points to his own temple.

"He ... stole it from me, I think. In the truck, yes- terday, when I was asleep."

Ollie stares at him with eyes that are confused and worried. Maybe even wary.

David's eyes, on the other hand, have an expression of shock that gradually moves into dread.

"So, what Walker said about Billy was right?" he says. "The collective consciousness and ..."

"Telepathy," Randall finishes for him, nodding. "I'm pretty sure Billy got the names of both Wiley and the sawmill from me. That he took them from my subconscious while I was asleep."

"Wait, wait, wait, hit the brakes," Ollie exclaims. "Are you telling me your son can read our minds? That he knows everything we do?"

"I ... well, no, I don't think so. He has to work for it, I think. Get us to ... let him in."

In a fleeting glimpse, he sees Billy, the way he stood in the dream with one foot pressed against the wall and both hands closed around the handle of the door into the school library's ARCHIVE. How he tugged and toiled to get it open, and how he finally gave up and turned his sad, heart-melting Bambi eyes at his father to ask for help—and got it.

"In the dream, he was trying to get into a room, an archive of some kind," Randall continues. "But the door was stuck, and he couldn't get it open, so I, um ..."

"So you helped him?"

Making eye contact with David and Ollie at this moment is difficult for Randall, but he forces himself to do so.

"I ... I'm really sorry, but I had no idea what the consequences would be. So yeah, I opened the door for him."

"I'm almost afraid to ask," Ollie says. "What was in there?"

"This," Randall sighs, gesturing at the burning sawmill. "There was a note with the name of the place ... and Wiley."

"So, this is where we're at," David says. "The scouts have been killed, we have no idea where the flock and Billy are—and maybe, just maybe, they know all about our plan."

"Fuck," Ollie exclaims, clenching his hand and pressing it against his forehead. "Fuck, fuck, fuck!"

"They could be anywhere," David continues. "We don't stand a chance of finding them. Hell, we've got no leads to go by. We don't even know if they're still in Colmena, and even if we did know, it would still be like looking for a—"

That's as far as he gets before Randall stops him by raising his hand.

"Maybe we *do* have a lead," he says, halfway to them, halfway to himself. "Maybe Billy, without even knowing, gave us one."

"What do you mean?"

"In the dream, we were in a place where I haven't been before," Randall says. "A school. I ... I saw its name when I walked into the library. What the heck was it?"

He closes his eyes and tries to find his way back to his old self—to the author who used to write down his dreams so he could use them as sources of inspiration for his stories. A habit that, over time, enabled him to recall more and more details when he needed to.

And he does now. More than ever.

Behind closed eyelids, he begins to paint a picture of the things he remembers from the dream: the empty playground, the windows into the classrooms, the whiteboard with the words DON'T CALL THE POLICE, and the swing set where he first saw Billy.

Feeling an echo of the panic he felt in the dream, he once again follows Billy through the school's long, semi-dark hallways, while doors and bulletin boards glide by.

He follows the sounds: the heavy scraping, as if someone is dragging a piece of furniture across a tile floor, and the sound of a child trying to lift something heavy.

And then, suddenly, it's there.

The sign.

"Ellie-May Kaufmann's Elementary," he says, opening his eyes. "They're at Ellie-May Kaufmann's Elementary."

"A school?"

Randall nods.

"I saw the name on the door to the school library. That's ... that's where I found him. I also saw a road sign with the name of the street where it was located. What was it? Something to do with a desert, I think, but I can't ..."

For a moment, his brain shuts down completely, and he feels a splash of panic at the thought of being so close and then dropping the needle back into the haystack.

Then it comes to him, clear and distinct in his head, like a neon sign on Broadway.

"Tumbleweed Crossing," he says. "The street was completely deserted and empty ... and it was ironic because it was called Tumbleweed Crossing."

For a while, neither of the others say anything. Then Ollie nods, slowly and thoughtfully.

"I guess it's worth a shot ... but we'll have to find another ride, I'm afraid."

As if on command, the three of them turn around and look toward a barn-like building next to the timber slide over on the right side of the driveway.

"The scouts must have had a car," Randall says. "So, if we're lucky ..."

Ollie and David nod simultaneously, both with the same hopeful look in their eyes. Then they start walking over to the building.

The entrance is a wide wooden gate, which, to their luck, hasn't been locked off with the padlock and the large chain hanging on one side.

And their luck extends beyond that, for as they

pull open the doors of the gate, they are greeted by the rear of a dark blue Subaru Outback station wagon.

"You wouldn't happen to be as good at short-circuiting cars as you are with a gun, would you, kid?"

David smiles at Ollie and shakes his head.

"No, for that you'd have been better off with Jerry from my chemistry class, I'm afraid. Pretty sure he knew how. But my dad had a car that looked like this one, so I might have an idea."

He starts walking around the car, stopping to put his hand under the body over each tire.

"What are you doing?"

"It's a long shot," David replies. "But my dad had this thing. A magnetic box with—"

"With what?"

Rather than answering with words, David pulls his hand out from the shadows above the left front wheel and throws something over to Randall.

It's a small, black box with a magnet attached to its back—and inside it is a spare key with the Subaru logo printed on it.

"I could kiss you, kid," Ollie says.

"Please don't."

With renewed—albeit cautious—hope, Randall walks over to the door on the driver's side of the car, puts in the key, and turns it.

A synchronous click sounds from both front doors, and he draws in some air through his nose, puffing it out through his mouth as he mumbles the words:

"So far, so good."

Having taken a seat behind the wheel, he repeats the ritual. This time, it's just two deep breaths he takes. Then he puts the car key in the ignition and turns it.

The Subaru coughs ... coughs again ... and then starts growling like a big feline.

"Fuck yeah," he hears David say, and it puts a smile on his lips.

"Then we just need to salvage what we can from the truck," Ollie says. "Will you drive this one over to it, so we won't have to carry the stuff all the way over here, Randall?"

"Yeah, no problem. "

With those words, Randall puts the Subaru in

gear and backs out of the gate. He then turns and drives over to the truck, which is still sitting under the canopy with its radiator grille gaping over the corner of a stack of logs as if it were trying to take a bite of it.

By the time he gets out of the Subaru, David and Ollie have already started unloading stuff off the bed of their former vehicle. They do it via the same rip in the tarp that David used to get out. Because even though the back part of the tarp and the door in the rear are no longer burning, the two things have merged into an obstacle that won't be easy to pass.

"The fire melted the bottles, so most of the water is destroyed," David says as he carries a box of cans over to the Subaru and puts it into the trunk. "But the food is okay, I think."

"Then we'll just boil some more snow," Randall says, shrugging. "At least we're good at ..."

He loses his train of thought, when, out of the corner of his eye, he sees Ollie approaching with a metal suitcase.

"I haven't seen that one before. What's in it?"

Ollie hesitates—too long for him to shy away from the question or dismiss it with a shrug—and then sighs.

"It's ... a tranquillizer gun. It was Walker's idea."

"A tranquillizer?" Randall replies, and he's on the verge of asking what it's for when he realizes the answer is obvious. So, what he ends up saying instead is: "That's probably a good idea."

Behind Ollie, David opens the passenger-side door of the military truck and leans over the seat. When he comes back out, he has a folded map in his hands.

"Well thought, David."

David responds with an absent humming sound, after which he walks over to one of the stacks they hid behind earlier. There he unfolds the map and lets his index finger slide around on the paper.

"Well, I'll be damned," he mutters, when his finger finally stops. Then he looks up at Randall. "To be honest, I didn't really believe it ... but you were right. It's right there, in the western part of Colmena. Tumbleweed Crossing. And if the road is there ..."

Randall isn't as surprised as David, but nonetheless, it all suddenly feels enormously overwhelming. Because he no longer has a shred of doubt.

Ellie-May Kaufmann Elementary School *is* located on Tumbleweed Crossing in Colmena ... and that's where Billy *is* at.

So, if everything goes according to plan, he will get to see his son again before this day is over.

part 3

THE SCHOOL

"*Revenge in the mind of anyone is a dangerous thing.*
Revenge in the mind of a patient man
is always worse."
—O. E. Geralt, Bad Bread.

chapter 13

Making the decision to wait until the sun had set was easier than actually doing it. But now that darkness has fallen and they are standing in an abandoned house in Colmena, staring at the school, fifty yards away, the impatience is long forgotten.

In fact, it all suddenly feels pretty rash and impulsive.

Also, there's another sensation that has the nerve threads in Randall's spine vibrating.

Déjà vu. The feeling of ... no, *the certainty* that the playground he sees over there is the same as the one he saw in the dream. That the swing he can see the contours of in the dark not only looks like but *is* the one his son sat on.

"I think something is happening," Ollie says. For a good while, he's been standing by the window along with Randall, looking for signs of life over at the school. "I think I saw someone who ... holy crap!"

"Someone who what?" David asks behind them, but Ollie flatly ignores him.

So does Randall—because now he's spotted it, too.

Children, hundreds of them, marching in unison across the street and then toward the school. Small, creepy silhouettes that alternately fade in and out, depending on whether they are hit by the light from the moon.

"Hey, I asked you a—"

David gets no further before seeing it with his own eyes and losing his voice, just like the other two.

"It ... it's like Redwater," he stammers as his ability to speak returns.

"No," Randall says, shaking his head. "There are more now. Many more."

Those words are allowed to hang in the air—and

with each second they do so, they confirm themselves even more.

For the flock of children continues to surge on the small street, then disappears behind the doors of Ellie-May Kaufmann's Elementary.

"How can they even ... *fit* in there?" David asks.

Randall's intention is to answer that he doesn't know, but the only thing leaving his mouth is a muddy *huh* sound.

For what feels like an eternity, the procession continues while Randall, David, and Ollie remain glued to the window. And then, strangely undramatically, it's over. The rearguard narrows in like a snake's tail until, in the end, it consists of only two children.

When these last two backstops have entered the school doors, Randall stays by the window for a moment, then takes a step back and sits down on the floor.

"Are you okay?" David asks.

"I didn't see him," Randall says. "And I ... I don't know if I'm relieved or sad about it."

"There were so many," Ollie says. "Your son may

well have been somewhere in the crowd if—"

"I know," Randall interrupts. "And he *is* in there, I know that too ... but I didn't see him."

Ollie starts to say something more, but David stops him by putting a hand on his shoulder.

"Ollie, would you mind keeping an eye on the windows?" he asks. "See if it calms down?"

Ollie looks at David, then down at Randall and back at David. Next, he nods and turns to face the window as David walks over and sits down next to Randall.

"Maybe I should go in there alone," Randall says.

"What are you raving about?"

"It's just ... what if Billy has tricked me again? If he knows we're coming and we get ambushed, then it will be my fault. Again."

"None of this shit is your fault, Randall. None of it. Besides, I gave you the rules a long time ago. Way back when we walked into the hospital in Newcrest. Remember?"

Randall looks at him, confused, but after a few seconds it comes to him, and he shrugs.

"Not some horror movie bullshit where we split

up. Was that it?"

"Close enough," David replies, placing his hand on Randall's shoulder. Then he—in a voice that makes him sound a lot older than he actually is—adds: "We're not going to change the plan now. We wait here and hope to God that Walker is right in that the hive mind also makes them rest at the same time. And when it's calm over there, Ollie will let us know. Then we sneak in and get Billy. Deal?"

"Deal," Randall says, nodding. "We'll wait."

And that's what they do. They stay in the house, taking turns keeping watch at the window—and when half an hour has passed—during which none of them have seen any signs of activity—they decide to leave the house.

Outside, they are embraced by a chilly wind carrying tiny, fragile snowflakes, which melt on their cheeks and hands. Fortunately, they find shelter upon crossing over to the opposite sidewalk, where they can walk alongside a tall fence.

"It's taken on a whole new meaning, huh?" David says, pointing up to a traffic sign by the last crosswalk before they're at the school.

BEWARE! CHILDREN CROSSING! it says.

"You can say that again," Ollie replies.

When they've gotten a little further, David pauses again. This time he doesn't point to anything. Instead, he squints his eyes and tilts his head.

"That creaking sound. What is that?"

"The swing," Randall replies without a shadow of a doubt. "It's the swing inside the playground. The wind is pushing it."

For a moment, David looks like he's about to ask how Randall can sound so sure, but then he just shrugs and moves on.

As they open the fence's gate and enter the playground, Randall's sense of déjà vu returns. Because apart from it now being bathed in the blue glow of the moonlight, everything is as it was. Even the ice crystals in the air seem to dance around him in the exact same pattern that they followed in the dream.

"I don't like this," David says, and both Randall and Ollie answer him with the same *you're not the only one* head shake.

"The sound is almost the worst."

No one asks Ollie what he means because they already know. And it *is* disturbing, to say the least, that all they can hear is the squeaking of the swing and the snow creaking under their shoes, when they've just seen an army of kids march into the school.

The entrance door has a large pane of frosted glass, and as he puts his hand on the handle, Randall's brain senses something behind that glass. More than anything, it's a premonition, fleeting and vague like an abstract painting, that sets off an alarm in his subconscious.

But as the door opens into the long, semi-dark hallway, that little alarm bell turns into a roaring siren.

The floor is filled with children. Small arms, small legs, and small faces everywhere. Like fish in a barrel, they lie on their backs in the dark, tangled together with no apparent order or structure. As if they at some point just stopped, toppled over, and fell asleep.

"Oh God," he hears someone say behind him, but the voice is too distorted to tell if it's Ollie or David.

Cautiously, making sure it makes as little noise as possible—and that it goes free of the boy lying closest—Randall pushes the door all the way open. Then he steps into the hallway.

There are spots where he can place his feet on the floor without touching any of the kids, but they're scattered, and it feels like tiptoeing across a minefield.

When he's gotten a few feet in, something touches his arm, startling him.

He turns around and sees David holding his hands apologetically up in front of him. Then he points at himself and Ollie and draws a semicircle in the air.

Randall understands the message—*maybe we should try another way*—and responds by shaking his head and pointing to a small window in the door to their right.

Behind the window is a classroom. In it children also lie everywhere, on the floor as well as the tables. David peeks in there, blinks in disbelief, and then, with a resigned nod, shows that he has drawn the same conclusion as Randall:

On this winter-cold evening, there is no path into the Ellie-May Kaufmann school that isn't paved with sleeping children.

With the others following right behind, Randall resumes his cautious walk through the eerie obstacle course, which becomes more challenging with each step because the light loses to darkness the further they move into the building.

They won't get far before that fight is over, with the darkness as the clear victor, meaning they'll have to take a risk if they plan to continue.

With that reasoning, Randall puts his hand in his jacket pocket, pulls out a lighter, and holds it up for the others to see.

Ollie looks at the lighter, checks that his gun is loaded, and nods. So does David.

Randall nods too. Then he takes a deep breath—and presses his thumb down on the lighter's ignition mechanism.

The flint stone sparkles, and a flame, small and weak, shoots forth.

For a moment, Randall's imagination insists that all the kids on the floor around him—whose faces he is now able to see—fling open their eyes at the same time, staring at him.

It's all in his head. None of them heard the sound, and no one is looking at them. They still lie completely motionless, confined in the trance-like sleep of the collective consciousness.

From the children, Randall's gaze slides up onto the wall, where a bulletin board is mounted. On it hangs a poster that chills his spine. It shows a black silhouette of a group of children standing on a hilltop, posing like superheroes. Below them is a simple and clear message:

ELLIE-MAY KAUFMANN'S ELEMENTARY.

WHERE THE LEADERS OF THE FUTURE ARE SHAPED!

He gulps, then forces his gaze away from the poster and back toward the floor. Then he signals to the others that it's time to move on.

Together, they move on down through the hallways, trying to navigate around the stream of pale, slumbering children gliding in and out of the fragile, flickering circle of orange light from the lighter.

At the end, they have two paths to choose from.

Randall decides to take the right one, which leads them past another long line of closed doors on both sides. It also ends with a door. One that is bigger than the others and carries a sign with the words SCHOOL GYM.

The door is slightly stuck, so he has to push harder this time to get it open. What he just hasn't realized is that the increased resistance is due to the hydraulic cylinder at the top, which causes the door to close automatically after use.

And when that cylinder retracts, it triggers a hollow, sucking sound.

All three of them freeze in place, and Randall instinctively removes his thumb from the lighter's gas button, thus killing the light.

Now they stand there, shrouded in darkness and a nauseating smell of children that is best compared to the one found at the end of the day in the ball pit of a playland.

Randall concentrates on listening, and when he realizes he can't hear anything, it only makes him even more uneasy.

Because before, he could hear the sound of the

children breathing. Like a faint sound carpet in the background, it lay; soft and eerily synchronous ins and outs.

But now, it's quiet. Not a sound can be heard.

Well, I guess that's it. You woke them up. Now it's only a matter of time before they start throwing themselves at you. You'll be buried in children, Randall, and it's your fault. Yours and yours alone.

Now there is something. A faint scrape, as if someone is moving uneasily ... but then the sound dies out and the children's calm breathing gradually takes over again.

Randall's own breath also returns, strained and unstable at first, then slower and more controlled.

When, after an uncertain period of time—it may have been a minute, it may have been ten—there still hasn't been any more changes to the rhythm of the children's breaths, he finds the courage to turn on the lighter again.

To his relief, the children's eyes are closed, and they stay that way, even as he starts to move on.

The finish line feels eerily close now. Maybe it's because they are approaching the center of the building, and he imagines that's where the leader will be.

Though he thinks this way, he jolts as they reach the opposite end of the hall and he spots the stage under a dusty beam of blue moonlight from a ceiling window.

Because unlike everywhere else in the school, the stage floor is not covered by children. On it, there's only one child—a fair-haired boy sitting in lotus position with his head bent slightly downward so most of his face lies in shadow.

But somehow—perhaps because the lighter's light is reflected in them—the eyes are still visible.

Billy's beautiful, ocean blue, wide-open eyes.

chapter 14

"Hi, Dad," Billy says—and when Randall, instead of answering, casts a nervous glance back at the kids on the floor at the foot of the stage, he adds: "Don't worry, they won't wake up until tomorrow unless I tell them to. You can talk."

On that point, however, the boy is awfully wrong. Randall *can't* talk. He can barely *think*. His mind feels like a wobbly house of cards—and the boy in front of him like the hurricane that will inevitably tear it apart.

Because there are countless ways in which he has imagined that this moment would play out, but none of them looked like this.

"Why, Billy?" David breaks in with a voice that sounds tormented, on the verge of crying. "Why did you do it?"

Billy tilts his head slightly and stares at him.

"Did what? The thing at the sawmill, the thing in Redwater, or something else? You'll have to be a little more specific, David."

"Rose never was anything but good to you," David says. "She took care of you. She ..."

His voice breaks, and the rest of the sentence fades into nothing, as if a volume button has been turned down.

Not that it seems to matter much, as Billy's interest is long gone. His attention is back on his father.

"I'm a little disappointed," he says. "I knew you'd show up at some point, but that it would take you so long ..."

He finishes the sentence by shrugging. Then he tilts his hand to the side as if to say: *But let's not worry about that anymore, no need to dwell on the past.*

"We can help you," Randall says. "If you'll let us, we can bring you to someone who—"

"But I don't need help, Dad. Look at me. I talk, I stand, I walk. I'm well. Isn't that what you wanted?"

"You're not well, Billy. You have a disease, but it

was never that you couldn't talk and couldn't walk. It's another disease. You have some parasites in your brain that ... manipulate you and make you do things. Things that you wouldn't have done otherwise. Bad things."

The boy pulls his lips up into a cryptic smile that Randall discovers he can see in the semi-darkness, even though the flame of the lighter at some point during their conversation has gone out.

"It would have happened anyway," Billy says. "All we did was speed up the inevitable."

"What are you talking about?" Randall asks, although he believes—and fears—that he already knows what the boy's answer will be.

"Death," Billy says. "It would have come to them sooner or later. Their bodies would give up. That's the way they're built. We just helped it along."

"No, Billy. This is not you. Oh God, don't say things like that."

"*They* were the ones who were sick, Dad. Not me, not us. Their disease is called *old age* and *death* ... and we don't suffer from that. We're immune."

"You're coming with us, kid," Ollie says. "If it's

the one way or the other, that's up to you, but I'm not leaving this school without you."

Billy stares at him with a rebellious look. Then he closes his eyes. A second later, a unanimous sigh passes through the hall, as if all the children see something in their dreams that makes them gasp loudly.

They don't wake up, but the message—that they would have if Billy had wanted them to—is resoundingly clear.

Billy apparently thinks so too, because now he goes back to ignoring Ollie as if he's not there at all.

Instead, he looks closely and oddly curiously at Randall. Almost as if he were a mysterious object that the boy has accidentally dug free while making a sandcastle on the beach.

A thought—a question that he's often asked himself—strikes Randall, and he instinctively knows it's important. That it is paramount that he puts it into words now.

"If it's sufficient justification that we'll grow old and die anyway," he says. "Then why did you make exceptions? Why did you spare me? And what about David? Why did he go free?"

Billy's eyes transform into small, thin lines, but he says nothing, and Randall can't determine if it's due to anger or an even stronger curiosity.

"He was an obvious target, sitting there on the stairs with Rose in his arms," Randall continues. "So why on earth didn't you shoot him?"

He pauses, partly to make the words extra powerful, and partly to get a proper hold on the reins of his own emotions so they don't run away.

"Do you know what I think?" he then says. "I think it's because my son is still in there. And I also think it was because of him that David and I escaped from Redwater alive."

"Or I chose to let you go free because I wanted you to suffer," the boy says. "Because I wanted you to know what it feels like to be let down the way you let me down. So you'd feel as lonely as I did when you let Mom drag me to Newcrest, without putting up a fight, because you'd rather sit in a cabin up in Maiden Lake and write books than be a father."

Don't listen to him. It's the parasites talking. Not Billy.

Entirely possible. But it's Billy's mouth the words are coming out of, and it's Billy's voice that conveys them. And they hit Randall like a battering ram in the solar plexus.

"Billy, I ... it wasn't ..."

"You didn't care about me," the boy continues. "When Mom got sick, you didn't even show up."

"I ... I didn't know ..."

"And where were you when police officers came and pulled me out of the apartment, huh? When they took me and all the other kids to the hospital, where were you?"

Randall's trachea is closed by the tsunami of guilty conscience that the boy's words are flooding him with.

But even if Randall had been able to answer, Billy would probably have preempted him—now that he throws the ace on the table and says:

"But what hurts the most is the secret that you think I didn't know about. That you found yourself a new son because the one you got back was broken."

Without wanting to—because it's an agonizing

confirmation that there's a grain of truth in what Billy is saying—Randall's eyes drift over to David. They don't stay there for long, though, because behind David there's something else that attracts them.

The kids on the floor. They have once again started to move uneasily.

"Did you really think I couldn't tell that David was your favorite?" Billy continues. "That I couldn't see how—"

A click and a loud hiss, like when you deflate a tire, interrupt the boy's monologue ... and instead of resuming it, Billy just stands still, staring, disoriented, into the air.

For a moment, Randall considers that the boy might have shut down, as he saw several of the blanks—including his own ex-wife—do in the beginning. Then he notices the little yellow tuft sticking out just above the boy's right collarbone.

The top end of a tranquilizer dart.

With large, perplexed eyes blinking slower and slower, Billy looks down at the arrow. Then he gradually tilts forward until he finally collapses completely on the stage floor.

There he remains in a fetal position while Randall, David, and Ollie skim the floor below the stage to see if any of the kids were pulled all the way out of their sleep. Luckily, that doesn't seem to be the case.

"I had to do it," Ollie says. "If they had woken up, we never—"

"I don't hold it against you," Randall replies. "You had no other choice."

As he speaks, he hands the lighter to David, after which he walks over to Billy and kneels beside him.

For a moment, he just stays there, staring at him. It feels like sitting in a graveyard, staring at a tombstone, not knowing if the one you're missing has a soul and is still able to hear what you want to tell them.

He also speaks to the unconscious boy in the same way that one often speaks to the dead: with words that never get out in the air.

Are you in there, Billy? If you are, know that I'm right here ... and I'm not going anywhere.

Carefully, he slides his hands under his son's

back and lifts him up. With the boy in his arms, he then gets back up and starts walking toward the stairs leading down from the stage.

"David, would you mind?"

"What? Oh, yeah, of course," David says, walking over to Randall and turning on the lighter.

"Thank you."

The walk back through the minefield isn't exactly easy, carrying Billy's limp body in his arms, but when Ollie offers to take over and relieve him a bit, Randall merely shakes his head.

Because he's Billy's dad, and that means this is something he has to do. That it's his task and his responsibility.

Outside, the playground is still lit up by the moon, even though the bluish glow from earlier has taken on a gloomy tinge of dark gray. The biting winter wind is also still there, although it's no longer filled with tiny snowflakes.

When they've made their way back to the driveway of the abandoned house from where they watched the school, Ollie signals the others to stop.

"I don't know about you," he says. "But after

seeing how that little guy controls those kids, I'm thinking we should drop the plan of spending the night in Tinfields and go back to Merryway instead. It's a long stretch this late at night, I know, but I for one would like to be as far away from here as possible when he wakes up."

Randall looks down at Billy and nods.

"I've been thinking the same."

"I think we all have," David adds.

"Alright then," Ollie says, pulling out the car key from his pocket. "Will you go get our stuff from the living room, David? We'll get this little fellow in the car in the meantime."

David nods, then runs over to the terrace door and disappears behind it. As soon as he's gone, Ollie turns to face Randall.

"I owe you an apology," he says.

"What for?"

"Complaining about you coming along on the mission. I badly underestimated you guys. Especially you. But I'm not going to make that mistake again. How you still have the strength to fight on, with all the shit you've been through, I simply don't understand. But I respect it."

Randall hesitates for a long time. Then he takes a deep breath and lets the air out in a long sigh.

"I don't really have much choice," he says, shrugging. "This is my son."

chapter 15

Waiting can be a very particular form of torture. Especially if you have no idea what you're going to get when the wait is over, except that it's probably going to be bad.

That's how it is for Randall right now, sitting in the back seat of the Subaru, staring at his son—or whatever it is—that's sitting beside him, sedated and with his hands tied together with duct tape.

Most of the time, the boy's head is leaned against the side window so Randall can't see his face, but occasionally the car hits a bump, causing Billy's head to tilt to the left.

When this happens, it usually only lasts a brief moment before his head falls back against the windowpane, but it's still enough to have an impact on

Randall.

For in those moments, he is thrown back to the time before Redwater, before the Collapse, and before the auditorium at Newcrest Memorial. Back to the time when he and Allie were still together, and where family trips usually ended with Billy sitting and sleeping the same way in the back seat, held up by the seat belt, head against the window.

In the front of the car, Ollie and David are also feeling the corrosive effect of the wait. They haven't said it directly, but Randall has seen them cast wary glances at the boy at shorter and shorter intervals.

And it's completely understandable. After all, it's been quite a while since they left the school in Colmena, so it won't be long before Billy opens his eyes—and since the spare tranquillizer darts were kept in another box which burned along with the military truck, they can't just knock him out again with one. Ergo, they'll just have to cross their fingers that they have gotten far enough away from Colmena to put Billy's slumbering army out of the range of his telepathic abilities.

"Would you mind taking out the map again, David?" Ollie asks. "I can't remember if I need to get on the 74 or the 68."

"The 68," David says promptly, but despite the confidence in his voice, he still pulls out the map and double-checks. "Yep, I was right. It's Highway 68 we need to get on."

He pauses and glances discreetly to the back seat.

"What, um ... what do we do when we get to Merryway?" he says. "With Billy, I mean. We'll probably need to ... secure him somehow, right?"

"I've been thinking the same," Ollie adds. Like David, he also sounds like he's testing the surface of the ice with his foot before every word.

"You don't have to sugarcoat it," Randall replies. "I'm his father, but I'm also aware how dangerous he is. And yeah, I've been thinking about it too. There wasn't a basement in your uncle's house, was there?"

Ollie shakes his head.

"No, but I'm pretty sure the garage can be locked from the outside and then we could take turns keeping watch."

Randall is on the verge of suggesting that he can do it alone, but he ends up nodding. Because all the good intentions in the world don't change the fact that it's been a killer of a day, and he's honestly not sure he'd be able to stay awake all night.

Outside, a row of cars glides by in the moonlight. If you didn't know any better, you could think that it was other drivers who were driving without lights and had been caught in a queue over in the opposite lane.

But Randall does know better. Those cars have been in that queue for years, and not a single one of them will make it to its destination. They're going to be stuck there until—

The thought is never completed, because next to Randall, Billy's fingers have begun to move, and the rhythm of his breathing also seems to have changed.

"Billy? Are you awake?" Randall hears himself say in a voice that, though he tries to downplay it, is soaked in a father's tenderness and worry. "Are you ... are you okay?"

Billy opens his eyes but doesn't answer. At least not verbally. Nevertheless, his face is twisted, and the expression in his gaze seems to carry an unequivocal message:

I hate you.

"We had to sedate you, Billy. You understand that, right? We had no choice."

No response.

"But it's for your own good, honey. We are going to take you to a researcher who thinks she can heal you. That she can make you well again."

I hate you, Billy's eyes repeat, maybe even with a dash of *I hate YOU ALL.* But his mouth remains closed.

"Billy, please ..." Randall begins, but then he makes eye contact with David, who shakes his head.

"We still need to drive for a good while," Randall says instead. "Try to see if you can get a little more rest, okay?"

The boy sends his father one last angry look and rolls his eyes ... but at least he then turns his face back to the window so that Randall gets out of the line of fire.

Maybe it's okay if Billy's new strategy is to sulk and give them the cold shoulder. It's certainly preferable if the alternative is another monologue like the one he gave at school, where he tried to explain why it's okay, *meaningful* even, to kill innocent people simply because they have the prospect of dying one day anyway.

They were the ones who were sick, Dad. Not me, not us.

Discreetly, Randall puts one hand over the other and squeezes, trying to drown out the thoughts with pain. The knuckles turn white, and it hurts all the way into the bones, but the desired result doesn't come. The echo of the things the parasites said inside the school gym, using Billy's vocal cords, still lingers in his head.

Their disease is called old age and death ... and we don't suffer from that. We are immune.

chapter 16

By the time David knocks on the wall behind him, announcing that it's time for a guard change, Randall has to admit that he probably would have lost the battle during the night, had he been on his own. For the last four hours of fighting to resist the siren song of sleep have been hard. And more than once, the door to the garage that he has been staring at has slipped in and out of focus.

"Anything new?" David asks.

"Nothing worth mentioning," Randall replies, sighing. "When he speaks, he alternates between being angry with me and acting innocent. Most of the time he's just been silent, though, like he was in the car ... and like he is now."

David shrugs, then holds out his hand. Randall

takes it and lets himself be pulled up from the chair.

"Call me if anything happens. Even if I'm asleep, you just wake me up."

"I will," David says, after which he slips into the chair, taking over the job of staring blankly at the door to the garage. "Sleep well."

"Thank you, and likewi... no, just thank you."

With those words, Randall leaves the small laundry room connecting the kitchen to the garage of the house that once belonged to Ollie's uncle.

Inside the living room, he spends his last energy throwing a few logs into the fireplace. When that's done, he staggers over to the couch and drops onto its cushions.

His sleeping bag has already been prepared for him, but he doesn't have the energy to crawl into it, so he settles for pulling it over him like a blanket.

With the crackle of fire and his own breathing as the only background noises, he lies still, watching the shadows' rippling dance on the wall. Each time the flames flare up, the shadows seem to devour a new piece of the wallpaper, and slowly but surely the darkness takes over.

But from the darkness a new light emerges.

A single, indistinct flame in the distance that gradually manifests itself and comes closer.

Something splashes under the sole of Randall's shoe as he takes a step backward. He looks down and finds that he is no longer lying on the couch but standing upright on a floor covered in water.

No. Not water. Water doesn't smell like that, and water doesn't have that rainbow-colored glow on its surface.

Oil? Gasoline?

He looks up again. The flame has gotten bigger, and now he can make out something underneath it. A bottle—and the hand that holds it.

The flame dances at the top of the bottle's neck, making it resemble an Olympic torch.

A frightening realization begins to dawn in his brain. If the burning bottle is an Olympic torch ... is its destination then the gasoline under his feet?

Panic creeps up through his nerve threads, and he tries to back away. He can't. His feet refuse to move.

As it approaches, the hand holding the bottle

slowly grows a body. First an arm, then a shoulder and a head, then a full torso, and finally a pair of skinny legs.

It's her. The girl from the sawmill, the one with the tangled pigtails. Somehow, she has returned from the dead to finish her task. To chuck a Molotov cocktail straight—

"Don't worry, Randall," he hears David say right next to him. "I've got a lock on her."

Something silvery appears on the edge of Randall's field of vision, and even before he has time to turn around to see it properly, the gun has been fired.

Bullseye. The bottle explodes, showering the girl with fire. She bursts into flames and collapses, screaming like a wounded animal.

But her burning body is no longer the only fire to behold in the darkness. Behind her, several more small, floating flames have appeared.

How many? Ten? Twenty?

A series of loud bangs, all followed by hideous snake hisses, reverberate in the dark as David starts shooting the new bottles as if they were targets in a fairground stand.

His sight is true, his mind unbending, and be-fore Randall has time to think, what's ahead is no longer a line of small, scattered flames. It's a wall of burning, screaming children.

The children run, stagger, crawl, and tumble around, in and out among each other, without or-der and without real hope, just as all the innocent people did during the Redwater massacre.

And just like them, they also eventually end up on the ground, squirming in pain until there is no more pain left to be felt.

One child is left standing when it's done. One child who has avoided the bullets and stubbornly keeps his flame intact.

He doesn't hold it above his head like the others did. He holds it in front of his chest, using both hands. In many ways, this boy looks like the kind of painting one would expect to find on a wall in a Catholic church.

As he and David begin to walk toward him, Ran-dall realizes that there's something else that's dif-ferent about the flame that this boy is protecting.

Because what this boy is carrying isn't a Molotov cocktail. It's a candle, and he—

Now the boy looks up, and ... oh God, it's him. It's Billy—and David has just raised his gun and locked his aim on him.

"D-Dad, help me," Billy says. His voice is weak and his pronunciation as uncertain as when he was in his wheelchair. "D-Dad, wake up! David wants to s-shoot me."

A click to the left of Randall's ear. The hammer on David's gun has been retracted.

"DAVID, NO!" Randall shouts, watching David's finger pull back the trigger.

The sound is a deep, rumbling bang that causes his eardrums to bend inwards and forces his eyelids to close.

When he opens them again, he's back in the living room of Ollie's uncle's house, where he jumps up from the couch and sprints toward the garage.

chapter 17

The chair in the laundry room is empty, the door to the garage is unlocked and open—and should Randall need more confirmation of his terrible foresight, he gets it, as he puts his hand on the door. For at that very moment, he hears David's voice, a distorted and shrill version of it, saying:

"No, no more! Whatever you have to say, I don't want to hear it, because it doesn't change shit. So just close your poisonous mouth and shut up, okay?"

"But David," Billy replies—with a voice so calm and innocent that Randall feels the hair on the back of his neck rise. "It wasn't me."

"You pushed her," David sobs. "*You* pushed Rose to her death, and *you* g-gave the order to shoot

Tommy and all the others."

"David!" Randall roars from the doorway. "For God's sake, David. Stop it! Put down the gun!"

David looks at him uncomprehendingly, as if he's unable to fathom how Randall even got into the room.

But he doesn't lower the gun. It keeps hanging in the air with the barrel pointed directly at the chest of Billy, who sits on a garden chair about three or four feet away from him.

"Randall, I … I thought I could, I really did, but I can't."

"What do you mean?"

"Him," David says, nodding towards Billy. "I thought I could let it go, for your sake, because he's your kid, but I can't."

"It was the parasites that made me do it, David," Billy says, a little too calmly and a little too unaffected. "They're in my head and I can't—"

"Shut up, Billy," Randall grumbles, though he doesn't believe it's actually Billy talking right now. "You're only making it worse."

"But Dad, he—"

"Shut up!" Randall repeats, while taking a cautious step forward and trying to make eye contact with David. When he has it, he raises his hands. "David, I'm begging you. This isn't the solution, and it's not you. You're better than this."

"Am I, Randall?" David asks. "Am I really better than this?"

Randall hesitates, longer than he should, but he can't prevent it. Because for a moment, that question throws two deeply disturbing slides up onto a film canvas in his mind.

One is David standing outside the broken window at the abandoned clothing store in Hollowfolk, staring at the little girl he just shot in the back.

The second is David standing under the half-roof of the sawmill with his arm resting on top of the log stack. In his hand, he has a gun, the barrel of which emits a thin line of smoke. The same gun he a second earlier used to blow up a Molotov cocktail so that its burning contents rained down on a girl in school uniform.

Am I, Randall? Am I really better than this?

"David, I ... I don't know. I don't know if there's

goodness left in any of us, or if we've been pushed, hunted, and deceived so much that there's no going back. But I do know that the last door will close if you pull the trigger now. You heard Walker. If you shoot Billy now, you risk cutting the last, thin lifeline humanity has left."

"Rose trusted him," David hisses through clenched teeth. "She *loved* him, Randall, and he killed her."

"We *all* trusted him, and we were all betrayed. Don't you think I've been where you are right now? You're not the only one who's been tempted to get revenge for Tommy, Rose, and all the others."

David stares at him with eyes that are wet, reddened, and full of doubt and shock.

"I'm not proud of it," Randall says. "But Billy also abused my trust, my love, and ... I've been there. But it solves nothing."

"He'll do it again," David sobs. "Don't you see? He will fool us. Make us think he's back to his old self and then, when we least expect it, he'll strike."

The last words are drowned in David's sleeve as he wipes a blend of tears and snot off his face with his free hand. The other hand is still pointed at Billy, but the gun's aim isn't stable anymore. The barrel dances up and down in the air.

"I can't let him do it, Randall. I can't. We can't trust him."

Randall looks down at Billy, halfway expecting to see an offended expression on his face, but the boy merely stares at them with curious eyes.

"I'm not asking you to trust *him*," Randall says. "I'm asking you to trust *me*."

As he speaks, he takes another few steps forward until he's so close to David that he could reach out and touch him if he wanted. But he doesn't. He keeps his hands calmly in the air in front of him.

"I'm asking you to believe me when I say it's *not* going to happen again," he says. "That I would never allow it. Even though he's my own son, I wouldn't let it happen. I *promise* you."

The words make David's face contract, first in bewilderment, then in an eerily agonizing expression. It's like watching a live version of Edvard Munch's *The Scream*.

And then, quite slowly, the gun starts to lower

until it's pointing down to the floor—and when Randall reaches out his hand to take it from him, David doesn't resist.

"Randall, I ... I don't know what got into me, I ..."

"It's okay. It's over now."

David looks at him with eyes full of shame and sadness.

"I miss her. I miss her so much."

"I know."

For a moment they stay there, in the middle of the floor of the garage, while the core of the problem—the little boy in the chair in front of them—sits and watches them with his strangely inquisitive eyes.

None of them say a thing. At least not until Ollie's voice sounds from the door behind them.

"What the heck happened here?"

"Nothing," Randall says. "I couldn't sleep because I had this nagging feeling that we hadn't locked the garage door properly. So, I asked David to help me check it."

Ollie squints his eyes and lets his gaze wander down to the gun in Randall's hand, from there onto

David, then Billy, and finally back to Randall.

"I see," he says. "And was it? Properly locked, I mean."

"Yeah. It was fine. I was just being overcautious. But better that than the opposite, am I right?"

Ollie nods hesitantly.

"Well, that's good then. How about I take the last shift now since I'm up anyway?"

"Yeah, that's probably a good idea."

part 4

THE LAB

"Well, look who's been a busy, busy little bee-atch!"

—*O. E. Geralt,* White Shadows.

chapter 18

In the afternoon of the next day, Randall sits in the back seat of the Subaru, staring out at the elongated concrete building that is an extension of the Ravens Congress Dam.

Five days. That's all it's been since he and David passed the dam the first time on their way to the research center, but it feels like a lot longer. Like something that happened in another life.

Something about that thought bothers Randall. Maybe it's because he still feels hollow and empty inside, even though he should be happy to have his son back. But the boy on the seat next to him also feels like something from another life. A mirage, with no real content.

"Oh, crap, not that one again," sounds from the

backseat.

Randall doesn't have to ask what David is referring to. He has seen it too, and he has no trouble remembering that the overgrown and icy wooden bridge didn't exactly thrill David.

Just as Randall himself did back then, Ollie lifts his foot off the accelerator when they reach the bridge, letting the car roll slowly.

The woodwork creaks disturbingly beneath them, but it's an empty threat, and the Subaru gets them safely over to the other side—and from there out onto Raven Road.

A little later, upon leaving a wooded area and driving into a small village, Randall has another flashback. This time, it's *Cliffsdale Baptist Church* whose name pops up in his head even before they're close enough to read the sign.

The first time they passed it, he only peripherally registered the hanged woman in the bell tower, but this time he sees her clearly—and suppresses a pretty absurd impulse to shield Billy from the sight.

"Two years," Ollie says as the lifeless woman grows smaller and smaller, then disappears out of sight in the rear window. "Two fucking years, and I still haven't gotten used to not being able to go anywhere without seeing shit like that. It's going to be good to get home."

Although his fellow travelers would hardly describe the research center as *home*—and while they rarely even raise an eyebrow at the sight of a hanged person—they both nod. Because if nothing else, Ollie is right about one thing. It will be good to get to the finish line.

Less than five minutes later, they catch the first glimpse of it. It doesn't come in the form of a suspended piece of vibrant-colored plastic tape, but rather the large wire fence that surrounds the research center.

"I'll open it," David says as Ollie stops in front of the guard shed next to the entrance gate.

Ollie nods, and David gets out, runs over to the gate, and pulls it open. Then he waits—with his shoulders pulled up to his ears and his hands lifted up to shield his face from the icy wind—while Ollie drives the car through the entrance.

When David gets back into the car after pulling

the gate shut, Ollie lets the car roll slowly in between the cluster of buildings that make ARL's area look like a small town. As he does so, he alternately flicks the car's headlights on and off.

"What are you doing?" Randall asks.

"I'm telling whoever is on guard duty not to throw flash bangs at us. We have an internal Morse code. A handy little trade secret."

Randall and David exchange a glance.

"We could have used that information when we arrived."

Ollie lets out a dry chuckle, but chokes it again almost instantly when he spots one of his colleagues further ahead.

The soldier stands at the end of the passage between buildings that they're in—and he doesn't exactly look like a candidate for Employee of the Month, standing there, leaned up against one of two bright green containers, just below the words *UNITED STATES ARMY PROPERTY*, so you'd think the text was referring to him.

As the car approaches, however, he does wake up a bit, and while Ollie parks in front of the white building to the right of the containers, the soldier strolls over to them.

"Hey, Ollie. New wheels?"

Astoundingly, it's only now that he hears the guard's voice that Randall realizes it's the same guard who welcomed them. The one who detained David ... and who, parenthetically, gave the impression of being a rather unpleasant person.

What the heck was his name ... Barney? Barley?

He doesn't have time to think any more about it before the answer comes from the driver's seat when Ollie says:

"Hey, Farley. Yeah, the truck got turned into a garden grill, I'm afraid. Will you let Walker know we've arrived?"

"Mm," Farley says as he leans down and looks into the back seat. "Is that him?"

"That's Billy Morgan, yes. Will you tell Walker we're back?"

"He doesn't look like much, huh?"

"And yet he's somehow wiped out half of Pennsylvania without breaking a sweat," Ollie replies dryly. "Will you please call Walker over the radio and tell her we're here?"

For a moment, Farley continues to stare at Billy with a mixture of fascination and fear in his eyes. Then he pulls back from the car door and nods to Ollie.

"Yeah, sure. I'll let her know."

"Thanks, Farley."

Farley nods again, then walks over to a small shed on the far side of the containers. In the meantime, Ollie turns to Randall.

"Sorry about that. I didn't mean to use your son as a scarecrow. It's just that sometimes you have to use the big chisel to hammer through that thick skull of his. Otherwise, he can stand there all day, doing nothing."

Randall nods and pulls his lips up into a smile that he doesn't feel sincerely. Contrary to what Ollie may think, though, it's not because he used Billy as a tool to scare Farley.

No, what's bothering Randall is that the scary story wasn't even made up. For Billy and his flock are indeed responsible for thinning out—on a pretty large scale at that—the current population of Pennsylvania.

Over by the shed behind the containers, Farley now reappears. He holds a walkie-talkie up to his ear with one hand and waves to Ollie with the other.

"There's a green light! You can go ahead and take the elevator down. Walker is waiting for you!"

Ollie replies with a two-fingered salute, then looks at Randall.

"Do you need help with him?"

Randall glances at Billy, who sits, still as a mouse, staring blankly at the gear lever, just like he has done during most of their trip.

"Nah, I'll manage," Randall says. "Besides, he still has his hands tied."

"It's not really his hands I'm worried about," Ollie says as he opens the door and gets out. "Just let me know, if you change your mind."

Before getting out, Randall puts his hand on Billy's shoulder and looks at him.

"Listen, I know this is probably the last place in the world you want to be, honey. But I promise it's for your own good. And you're in the best hands.

This place is full of brilliant people."

Since the boy has stubbornly maintained his silence for hours, Randall expects no answer—so when he gets one, it completely baffles him. Not least because the words—and the calm they are delivered with—give him the chills.

"I know, Dad," is what Billy says. "Otherwise, I wouldn't have come."

Outside, all four of them walk to the other side of the building, where they take the freight elevator down to the subterranean part of the research center.

As the elevator doors slide apart downstairs, Helen Walker's bright, curly hair and hazel eyes are the first thing Randall sees, and for a fraction of a second he feels a greater sense of hope than he has in a long time.

But it's only allowed to live for a fleeting moment before it starts to crack. Before the confusion—and then the sensation of having walked right into a trap—replaces it.

Because as she stands there in the corridor, welcoming them, Walker is not alone. She has brought along a welcoming party.

More specifically, six armed soldiers.

chapter 19

"What is this, Helen?" Randall asks, but the woman to whom his question is directed doesn't even seem to register his presence. Her focus is on Billy, who she now bends down to in order to make eye contact.

"My name is Helen Walker," she says with an educational, almost tender tone in her voice. "You have no idea how pleased I am to see you, Billy Morgan."

Billy doesn't say a word, but his eyes, small and cold, get the message through clearly: the feeling is *not* mutual.

"Helen," Randall repeats. "What's the point of all this?"

Walker looks up at him and then at her armed

entourage, standing in a semicircle around them. Then she shrugs and smiles her disarming smile.

"Oh, these guys? It's a precaution, nothing more. After all, we didn't know how ... challenging the situation would be."

She tries to make it sound like it's Billy she's worried about—even emphasizing it by peering down at him as she speaks—but something gives Randall the feeling that that might not be the case.

"But as you can see, we've got it under control," Ollie says. "So, perhaps the boys could find something more productive to do. Shoveling snow out at the front gate, maybe? It's needed."

Walker smiles at him ... but she doesn't tell her armed companions to back down, nor does she send them out to shovel snow. In fact, she doesn't say anything to them. She just turns to Billy again.

"I don't know how much your father has already told you, but I'm a researcher here and I'd really like to get to know more about you, Billy. About how you survived when all the other kids didn't. Would that be okay?"

Billy still doesn't answer, but a slight change

occurs in his eyes. The hateful gaze is laced with something else. A kind of demeaning glee. He looks like a school kid trying to suppress a giggle because the one he's talking to has a note on his back, saying: *KICK ME!*

"He can't talk?" one of the guards behind Walker asks.

"Can, but won't," she replies, looking up at Randall, who confirms with a reluctant nod. Then she puts her hand on Billy's shoulder. "We just need to get to know each other first, I think. Would you like to see my lab? I have all sorts of fun stuff. A super microscope, for instance. Then you can see a virus that can break-dance. Or find out if there are small animals living on a hair from a rabbit."

Again, Walker speaks in the sugary-sweet voice that, for some reason, makes Randall curl his toes.

He looks over at David and reads in his eyes that he has been thinking something similar.

She knows what he is. Why is she talking to him like that?

"It's been a long drive," Ollie says. "Maybe we should take a little break before we give him the grand tour?"

Walker gives him a defiant look, but then smiles and nods.

"You're absolutely right, Ollie. Why don't you go with Jameson over to the game room and take a breather? You've earned it."

"With Jameson?" Ollie stares at her, unable to hide his bewilderment—nor the fact that he's skeptical of the motive behind the suggestion.

"Really, that goes for the two of you as well," Walker continues, looking at Randall and David. "It must have been a tough couple of days for you guys too."

"We're used to being out there," Randall hastens to say, but Walker just shrugs and tilts her head slightly.

"I understand that it's not easy to trust others with such responsibility, but I think it would be best for all parties if Billy comes with me. Then you can take a well-deserved rest in the meantime."

"Well, that's not going to happen," David says.

"I'm afraid I have to insist," Walker says, glancing over at two of the armed soldiers. "Norris,

Pittmann, would you be so kind as to make sure that Randall and David get a nice, quiet place where they can rest a bit while Jameson takes Ollie over to the game room?"

The two soldiers step out of the half-circle and walk over to David and Randall, while the last one, who must be Jameson, places himself next to Ollie. All three have their hands parked on the grips of their machine guns and a *don't even try it* look in their eyes.

"You can't be serious!" Ollie protests. "We risked our lives to bring him here!"

"I know," Walker says. "And believe me, I wish we didn't have to do it like this."

She pauses, takes a deep breath, and shifts her gaze over to Randall.

"I really do mean it," she says. "But I have no other choice."

With those words, she puts her hand on Billy's back and gently leads him forward, away from Randall. The boy follows along without protesting. However, some distance down the corridor he pauses to look back over his shoulder and make eye contact with his father one last time.

And to send him a cryptic look that makes Randall's flesh crawl because it looks almost identical to the one the boy gave Walker earlier. The one that said:

I know something you don't.

chapter 20

"This way," Norris or Pittmann says—Randall still hasn't managed to determine who's who—after which he waves them into a room whose door he's just unlocked by entering a code in the panel on the wall.

A nice, quiet place where they can rest a bit.

Those were Walker's exact words, but Randall isn't really surprised to see that it's a room without windows and without escape routes.

Two collapsible camp beds are the only pieces of furniture, and the sight of them only confirms Randall's suspicions. The decision to separate them from Billy and lock them up in here wasn't impulsive. Walker had planned it.

"This just isn't happening," David says as he sits

down on the edge of the bed, buries his face in his hands, and lets out a frustrated growl.

"I'm afraid it is, kid," Norris or Pittmann replies. "But if it's any consolation, I don't think you're going to stay in here for that long. Just until Walker has finished her project."

"Her *project* is my son," Randall snarls. "You do realize that, right?"

"I think his status as a mass murderer trumps that detail," the soldier says dryly, before extending an open hand to David.

"What?"

"The gun I saw under your jacket earlier," the soldier says.

David adopts a perplexed facial expression, but then changes his mind and rolls his eyes as he pulls out the gun.

"You'll get it back if you behave," the soldier says as David drops the gun into his palm. "Do you have anything else? And I will find out, so don't try to bullshit me."

"That's all we've got on us," Randall says. "I had a Smith & Wesson, but if you want it, you'll have to go outside. It's in the glove compartment of the car we came in."

The soldier stares at him suspiciously for a while before finally nodding. Then he turns on his heel and waves his colleague with him toward the doorway.

"We'll come back with some food for you later."

"A Big Mac combo for me, please," David says as he gives the finger to Norris and Pittmann's backs. "With the thin fries and a large, regular Coke. None of that Zero shit."

"Dream on," one of them answers, just before the door shuts and the lock bolts shoot in with a *ka-klank*.

"Fucking assholes."

"They're just following orders," Randall says, mostly because that sounds like the sort of thing one should say. In reality, he doesn't disagree with David's choice of words.

"Orders, my ass. No one told them that the world ended?"

David keeps talking, but Randall only listens just enough to be able to nod at the right places. Other than that, he simply lets the young man's frustrated monologue be a backdrop for his own thoughts.

In particular, there are two questions he can't let go: what is Walker's actual plan for Billy, and why didn't Billy resist when she took him away?

The answer to the first question may be obvious. Perhaps Walker is simply nervous that Randall would change his mind at the last minute and refuse to let her examine Billy. But from that to showing up with six armed soldiers and placing both him and David in an improvised prison cell? It seems too drastic, too unwarranted. There has to be more to it.

The second question, Billy's undramatic surrender, he has a better guess at, though he really hopes he's wrong.

The problem is, though, that he is getting more and more confident that he isn't. For the look Billy had in his eyes as he glanced back over his shoulder out in the corridor, Randall has seen before.

In Redwater, up on the platform. It was right after Billy had pushed Rose over the edge and down onto the concrete stairs, and just before he raised his hand and ... *oh God*.

Randall jumps up from the camp bed, walks to the door, and starts knocking frantically on it.

"Hey! Norris, Pittmann, somebody, come back! We need to speak with Walker. Now!"

"What's going on?" David asks.

"He's done it again."

"Uh ... what?"

"Billy," Randall elaborates. "Did you see how he looked at Walker earlier—and at us, just before she took him away?"

In a matter of seconds, David's face undergoes a transformation in three steps, going from confusion to dawning comprehension and finally to horror.

"But they're ... *kids*," he says. "They can't have caught up with us so quickly."

"Not the group from Colmena, no," Randall says. "But there are also plenty of children scattered around Maryland. Like the girl who attacked me in Hollowfolk. And if Billy has spent the entire trip here sending ... information out to them, they know all about this place."

"Fuck."

"Yeah, fuck," Randall says, returning to his desperate knocking on the door. "Hello! Is anyone there? We need to talk to Helen Walker! To warn her. This entire place may be in danger. Is there anyone out there?"

No answer, not now, not half an hour later, when Randall and David finally give up and sit down on the edge of each of their beds, staring at their tender, bruised hands.

chapter 21

The first affirmation is the alarm. A loud, piercing wail that starts deep, rises in pitch, and then dies out for three or four seconds before starting over.

The next affirmation is the sound of sporadic explosions and outraged voices that are far away but still find their way down to Randall and David's makeshift cell via the vent ducts.

It would be a flat-out lie if Randall claimed he was surprised to hear these sounds, as he's been waiting for them ever since they get locked into this room ... how long ago? Two hours? Three?

But the fact that he isn't surprised doesn't stop the sounds from making the cold sweat of panic cover the back of his neck like a damp cloth.

For he, as well as his companion, who sits on the

other bed, tapping his foot uneasily, is fully aware that they are utterly defenseless in this small, locked room. If he's right, and it's the kids who have attacked the research center—and if the murderous youngsters were to claim the victory—he and David can, at best, hope to get shot at point-blank range in their cell. At worst, they'll starve to death.

"What do we do if they come down here?" David says. "We need to have a plan."

In a sarcastic and gloomy moment, Randall is tempted to answer what he's just thought—*get shot or starve to death*—but he bites his tongue, shrugs, and instead says:

"You hide behind the door. Hopefully I'll then be able to distract whoever comes in, long enough for you to overpower him. If only we had a ... wait."

He leans to the side and turns his upper body so he can peer down under the camp bed; more specifically, on the square aluminum tube that makes up one of its four legs.

"We can use this as a club," he says, then gets on his knees in front of the bed, grabbing the leg with one hand and the edge of the bedframe with the other.

The metal creaks and screeches as he begins to twist the leg from side to side, but the bolted clamp at the top doesn't open sufficiently for him to pull it off.

"Give me a hand, will you?"

David nods and walks over beside him. But when he grabs the leg and starts pulling, it quickly becomes clear that the result remains unchanged.

"If we flip it upside down, maybe? Then I can step on the frame while you twist the leg."

Randall looks at the bed for a moment. Then he grabs the edge of the frame, lifts it up, and tilts it around.

"I think it's working," he says after the first three or four hard pulls. "The clamp is opening."

"I see it," David replies. "Try moving your hand, so I can give it a kick."

Randall hesitates for a moment, glancing up at the grate covering the vent duct. Is it going to be too loud, thereby revealing them?

No, he doesn't think so. Besides, should anyone hear, they'll probably just think they've started pounding on the door again. Moreover, the sound of bangs and startled voices has only increased in volume, so it's doubtful that anyone will hear this.

With that reasoning, he removes his hand from the bed and nods up to David.

The first kick pulls the ends of the clamp apart, leaving an opening of about half an inch. The next kick opens it further, loosening the clamp so much that the leg now hangs on the frame at a 45-degree angle.

Third kick is the charm. The clamp opens completely, and the bed leg slides across the floor.

Randall picks it up and hands it to David, who whacks it against his palm a few times and nods.

"Now, we just need to wait," Randall says, and once more his gaze finds its way up to the vent grate. "Listen and wait."

And that's what they do. They sit down, Randall on the floor, David on the edge of his camp bed, listening intently to the noises resounding in the ventilation system. Noises that gradually become more uncomfortable—louder bangs, more panicked screams—with each passing minute.

How much time passes while they sit there remains unknown, but one thing is for certain: whatever is going on out there, it's getting closer. Because the sounds no longer just come from the grate. They come from the walls on all sides, footsteps and confused shouts. Even the wailing of the alarm seems to have gotten closer.

Both of them jolt when somewhere, very close, a loud bang sounds; the unmistakable sound of a gun being fired. Right after, a door opens and a series of quick footsteps clatter past right on the other side of the wall.

They look at each other, say nothing, but are probably listening for the same thing.

And then it comes, a voice that utters some sounds, which might be words, but might also just be frustrated outbursts.

It hardly matters, though. They've heard the sound of a voice—and confirmed that it's a *man's* voice, not a child's.

David is first on his feet. He jumps up to the door and pounds frantically at it with open palms.

"HEY! LET US OUT!"

Silence.

"WE CAN HELP YOU," David continues. "BUT YOU HAVE TO LET US OUT FIRST!"

More silence. Then a beep out on the other side of the wall. And one more.

"I think he's unlocking the door," David whispers.

Randall stares at him, nonverbally ordering him to hide behind the door, after which he pushes himself up so he can jump over and snatch the improvised weapon—that David has forgotten over on his bed—and throw it to him.

The last beep sounds at the exact second when David's fingers close around the bed's leg. Then the locking bolts are retracted with a hard clank, and the door opens.

chapter 22

Had they had more than a handful of seconds to react, Randall and David might have approached it differently. At the very least, they probably would have considered whether the person who unlocked the door after they asked to be let out might have good intentions.

But time *was* short, and when the door opened, David didn't hesitate for a second before kicking it back at full force, causing the person in the doorway to stumble backwards so fast that Randall only barely managed to perceive that the man was wearing a soldier's uniform.

And now, when David—roaring like a wild beast—leaps forward and knocks the bed leg into his back, Randall still can't see the soldier's face.

He can, however, hear him let out surges of moans between each blow—and they tell him what David only realizes later, after the fourth or fifth stroke, when his victim manages to put out some actual words.

"Hell, kid. Would you stop? It's me!"

David hits the brakes on the next blow but doesn't manage to stop it completely before the bed leg hits the man's back one last time.

"Ollie?"

"Yeah, god damnit," Ollie grunts, pushing David's leg, making him take a step backward. "It's me. What a fucking welcome."

"I ... I'm sorry, we thought ..."

"I know what you thought, kid. Are you guys okay?"

"We're okay," Randall says as he walks over to Ollie and helps him to his feet. "What about you?"

Ollie brushes his shoulders and sighs.

"Aside from the fact that I've just gotten the crap beaten out of me—thank you very much, David— I'm okay. They locked me up, but I managed to escape during the commotion. But hell, it's a freaking warzone up there. It's—"

"The kids," Randall finishes for him. "Billy tricked us again."

"Sadly, yes," Ollie says. "He's not dumb, that little punk. You have to give him that."

He pulls a gun from his chest holster and hands it over to Randall. Next, he turns to David and nods towards the bed leg in his hand.

"You'll have to make do with that one for now, but there's a weapons cache one floor up. We can find a gun for you there. We're going to need it if we want to get out of here alive."

"I'm not going anywhere without my son," Randall says.

"Yeah, I kind of figured you'd say something like that," Ollie sighs. "But have you thought it through?"

"What do you mean?"

"Have you thought about what's going to happen afterwards? You get Billy out, and then what? He's still a threat, a magnet that attracts murderous children."

It's probably not his intention, but the truth can

hurt, and right now, Ollie's question feels like an attack. One that hits Randall so cleanly that he has to suppress an urge to punch him.

"Right now, it doesn't matter if I know what happens afterwards," he says. "But I can tell you one thing that I *do* know. I know something is very wrong in this place, and I know Walker gave up the right to examine Billy when she locked us up. And no, maybe I don't see the plan as clearly as I'd like, but I know that what's best for Billy is to get out of here. Then we'll have to decide on the rest later. Besides, I think we can all agree that the kids running around the base right now shouldn't have the opportunity to get him back."

Ollie stares at him for a long moment, biting his lip. Then he finally nods and waves them along, muttering:

"I just know I'm going to regret this. You better keep up."

Randall and David nod, then follow him out through the door.

Out in the hallways, the rhythmic wails of the alarm are even louder, and as an additional stress factor, there are lamps flashing red on the walls, mounted with about ten yards' distance between each.

Bathed in their dark red glow, Ollie leads the way, taking them in and out through corridors and rooms, while panicked voices constantly scream and shout somewhere on a higher floor.

"It all looks the same," David groans as they round a corner and enter a hallway that could easily be mistaken for either of the previous two they've been in. "Are you sure we're not just running in circles?"

"I know the way," Ollie replies. "You just concentrate on keeping up."

"Okay, okay. I'm just making sure that you—"

David gets no further before a door opens at the end of the hallway in front of them. Out of it steps the soldier who was on guard duty with Ollie when Randall and David arrived.

And the expression on his face—a mixture of surprise and indignation—reveals that he recognizes them.

"Farley," Ollie says, holding out one hand in

front of him. "Don't do anything rash."

"Those two were supposed to be locked up," Farley stammers. "And ... so should you, Ollie."

As he speaks, Farley squints down at the gun in Ollie's other hand, and in a fluid, almost indiscernible motion, his own fingers find their way down to the gun holster at his belt.

"I can't allow you to leave with them," he says, pointing over to Randall and David. "All of this is their fault. You know that?"

Ollie shakes his head and takes a step forward. Then another.

"Farley, please listen. Randall and David have done nothing that Walker herself didn't ask them to do. She wanted Billy Morgan, and they ... no, *we* got him for her. Randall and David couldn't possibly have known this was going to happen."

Farley stares at Ollie with an expression in his eyes that Randall really doesn't like. He looks like prey that's been cornered and is now contemplating whether it's time for fight or flight.

"Bullshit," he mutters, at first faintly and nervously, then louder and more accusatory. "They knew, alright ... and you probably did, too. You probably have your brains full of fucking parasites too!"

"FARLEY, NO!" Ollie shouts, but it's too late. Farley has drawn his gun.

The first bullet hits the wall behind them, knocking off a large chip of concrete. The next grazes Ollie's left upper arm, sending him backwards, stumbling and bumping into Randall just as he's about to shoot.

The result is that the bullet from Randall's gun, which should have rendered Farley harmless, instead ends up in the warning lamp on the wall to his right.

There is, however, an upside to this failed shot as it extinguishes the enervating red flashes of the lamp once and for all.

Furthermore, the semi-darkness gives David enough cover—and perhaps courage—to dash forward and hammer the bed leg down on Farley's wrist.

Farley screams, staring in disbelief at the gun, which is knocked out of his hand and now slides across the floor of the hallway until it stops under Randall's shoes.

And that's the last thing he sees before David swings his aluminum club once more and knocks him out.

"I've never liked that jerk," groans Ollie, who is now sitting on the floor with his back against the wall and his hand pressed against his bleeding upper arm. He closes his eyes and lets out a hoarse, chuckling laugh. "I knew he was probably going to shoot me one day, but I always thought it would be by accident."

"Can you give me his belt, David?" Randall asks.

David tilts his head in confusion and points his thumb at Farley as if to say: *Farley's belt? Are you being serious?*

Randall nods down toward Ollie's arm.

"To stop the bleeding."

"Oh, yeah, sure."

David checks that Farley is unconscious, then turns him around, pulls off his belt, and brings it to Randall.

"Seems you got yourself a gun anyway, huh,

kid?" Ollie says.

"Yeah, he's not getting it back, that's for sure. But I've got to admit I've grown fond of my bed leg."

Ollie gives him a strained smile ... but it's ripped off his face again immediately when Randall tightens the belt.

"How does it feel?"

"Like I've stuck my entire goddamn arm into a hornet's nest."

"Good. It'd be worse if it was numb. But you were lucky, I think. It's bleeding a bit, but it looks as though it only grazed your arm. Do you need a hand?"

Ollie responds by getting up using his unhurt arm and starting to walk down the hall.

"The stairs are right over there," he says. "Are you coming?"

Randall and David look at each other. Then they get up and follow him.

chapter 23

When they've made it to the next floor—a mazelike tangle of hallways that look like all the others and are illuminated by the same flashing red lights—they agree that it's worth checking the weapons cache, even though David technically has a gun now. If nothing else, it wouldn't hurt to get a little extra ammo.

The room that the cache is in is not very large. In fact, the gun cabinet in itself takes up more than half the space.

Nevertheless, it is the furniture next to it—and especially what is standing on it—that catches their attention from the get-go.

The furniture is a small desk on which two monitors stand. Each of their screens is divided into four sections, showing live feeds from different surveillance cameras around the research center.

"This is *not* good," Randall hears David say behind him—and he agrees wholeheartedly.

About half of the feeds on the screens show empty corridors and rooms, but the other half show images that could be from nightmares.

At the top right, a man is running through a hallway. He has both arms in the air, and they are, along with the rest of his body, in flames.

Two squares to his left, two children are straddling a fallen soldier, whom they take turns stabbing in the back with knives.

Below them is the reverse scenario: two adult soldiers standing in a hallway, emptying their magazines into the back of a boy who looks to be no more than seven or eight years old.

All of these things play out behind the grainy, black-and-white filter of the screens, but somehow that just makes everything worse. Maybe because it feels grounded, like the shaky, handheld camera did in the *Blair Witch* movie when it came out.

But this doesn't just *feel* real. It is.

"We ... need to get a move on," Ollie says in a voice revealing that he's on the verge of throwing up. "We can't stay here, staring at that shit."

Randall nods but finds that he's having a hard time moving his gaze away from the screens. So hard that he has to reach out his hands and physically turn the monitor away before he succeeds.

"Good idea," Ollie says, after which he pulls a bundle of keys out from his pocket, turns to the weapons cabinet, and unlocks it. Once, he almost drops the key, but apart from that he doesn't seem too bothered by his injured arm.

Behind the cabinet doors are three drawers and a large, dark gray metal plate, covering the back wall. On it hang two pistols and an automatic rifle, but the first thing Ollie reaches for is a set of walkie-talkies standing below them.

"Here, take one each and set them to the same channel. Just in case."

While Randall and David set the walkies, Ollie pulls out one of the drawers and picks up two boxes of ammo.

"This should keep us going," he says and starts

to close the cabinet again. However, the doors don't close all the way before he changes his mind, opens them again, and pulls the automatic gun down from the metal plate. "Okay, I'm ready."

From the armory, he leads them to a new room—a break room with scattered tables and chairs, and a vending machine that's completely empty. From there, they step out onto yet another long, red-flashing corridor.

"There's a staircase at the end of this one," Ollie says. "It will take us up to the floor where Walker has her lab ... but you should probably expect there to be a lot of people up there. Especially if they're examining your son."

"And they won't be happy to see us," David says. "Is that your point?"

"Something like that, kid."

"We'll be careful," Randall says.

When they've reached the stairs and taken the first few steps, Ollie stops again, this time to take out one of the ammo boxes he found inside the weapons compartment and share its contents with the others.

"As soon as that door goes open, expect all hell to break loose," he says, pointing to the end of the stairs. "So, we enter, get the kid, and get out in a hurry. Deal?"

He waits for a nod from both of them, and when he has gotten it, he starts walking again. And this time, he doesn't stop until he's made it all the way up to the door.

"In, get kid, out," he whispers, placing his hand on the doorknob.

"In, get Billy, out," Randall and David repeat.

And then Ollie pushes open the door.

chapter 24

"What the hell? It's ... empty?"

Randall, feeling just as confused as Ollie sounds, looks at him and then back at the long hallway. It's the same as the one they were brought in through, when they met Walker and Andrews for the first time. Back then, there was life in this hallway and people to be seen inside the labs behind the windows on both sides. Now there are no people in sight, neither the kind in white coats nor the kind in military uniforms.

"Where is everybody?"

"I don't know," Ollie replies. "I guess they must have run away because of the fighting."

"But there are no kids here," David says. "And there's no sign of the kids even having been in this section at all."

David is right. There is nothing indicating that there has been a fight here. It's just empty—and that realization spawns a troubling idea in Randall's mind.

"Right or left?" he says, and without giving Ollie a chance to answer, he repeats it, louder and more aggressively. "Walker's lab, Ollie. Right or left?"

"L-left. Left, all the way down to the end and then to the right."

Randall nods and starts walking down the corridor, surrounded by windows that reflect him in a - bloody, red version every time the warning lamps light up.

Upon reaching the end, he follows Ollie's instructions and turns right, which leads him into a new hallway with more windows. However, this one does—without him being able to put his finger on why—feel more familiar, and he hasn't taken many steps before he sees the sign on the door.

LABORATORY, BIOCHEMISTRY A2.

Who are you trying to fool? Allie taunts. *Look around. Everything and everyone have left the sinking ship. He's not in there. You've lost him again.*

"Randall, are you okay?" sounds from behind him. "Why are you stopping?"

"Yeah, David. I ... I was just waiting for you guys."

"Oh ... okay. Well, we're here now."

Randall nods, forcing his feet to move again.

The door handle is plastic but putting his hand on it requires so much effort from Randall that you'd think it was burning hot metal.

He presses down, pushes—and has his worst fear confirmed. No scientists, no surgeons, no soldiers, no Walker ... and no Billy.

"NO!" he roars as he watches his fist collide with the door frame—a clash that should have triggered a wave of pain in his hand but which he can barely feel right now.

A hand touches his shoulder. His first impulse is to push it away, but he can't find the strength to do so. Its weight feels way too heavy. Like a sandbag over his neck, slowly but surely pushing him to his knees.

"Hey," David says. "We'll find him, okay? Do you

hear me, Randall? We *will* find him!"

Randall nods, but his legs still feel immovable, as if he had sunk to hip height in quicksand, and he has to lean on both David and the door frame to get up.

When the worst silvery spots in his field of vision have disappeared, he lets go of David's arm and moves on through the lab.

On the way, he passes the row of glass jars in which dead UPP-parasites are displayed, as if they were part of a butterfly collection. When he first saw these, he was fascinated and frightened, but now he barely notices them. His focus is solely on his next stop, Walker's office, where he hopes to find clues to Billy's whereabouts.

Leaving the parasite exhibit, he continues into a narrow passage between two racks with lab equipment, and as he reaches the end of it—and thus the door into Walker's office—he doesn't hesitate to enter. He knows that doing so would increase the risk of a new, and perhaps worse, nervous breakdown.

The office is just as messy as it was earlier. Piles

of paper and folders on the desk, sticky notes all over the side of the filing cabinet, and the two pieces of clothing on the armrest of the chair haven't been moved since last he was here. Even the two scans of parasite-infected brains are still hanging on the light board.

He starts with the filing cabinet, pulling out the top drawer and flipping through its folders.

Nothing useful.

Next.

Nothing useful.

Next.

Fuck!

He turns around and starts rummaging through the stacks of paper on the desk.

Lots of reports and newspaper clippings about parasites, about police assaults, about other kids, about fucking anything but ... wait.

BILLY MORGAN.

He runs a quivering finger across the name and down the edge of the thin cardboard folder. Then he opens it.

A single sheet of paper. That's all the folder

holds. On it are two illustrations, surrounded by small passages of text, some typewritten and others added in handwriting.

Both illustrations depict the same boy. He is unnamed, but age and physical traits reflect Billy's. One image shows the full-size boy, apparently strapped to a table or bed, while the other is a close-up of his neck and head. In both drawings, two small circles have been added to the boy's forehead. These circles are connected by some curvy lines to numbers and symbols scattered on the right side of the paper.

The same numbers and symbols recur in a mathematical formula further down, but it makes no sense to Randall. However, he doesn't like the conclusion that someone has added with a ballpoint pen below: *50-150 mA = outer limit for amplification of TP-signal. Starting point of short circuit.*

"What the hell are they planning to do to him?" David says, looking over Randall's shoulder.

Randall hears him but doesn't answer. He's too preoccupied with trying to extract meaning from the bottom-left text box.

*The greatest likelihood of success appears to be us-
ing the anterior cingulate cortex as an entry channel
and with limited anesthesia, as the empirical evidence
shows that sedation inhibits both host and remaining
parasites, resulting in a diminished effect.*

"Your dad was a doctor," Randall says—aware
that he spits out the words as if it were an accusa-
tion—and hands the paper to David. "What does all
this Latin shit mean?"

David skims the paper and then shakes his head
resignedly.

"I ... I can go out and ask Ollie if it means anything to him."

"Yeah, do that," Randall sighs. Then he turns
around again and continues searching through the
paper stack.

When David leaves from the office, all Randall's
remaining hope seems to do the same. He lets go of
the papers, puts his hands flat against the surface
of the desk, grinds his teeth together, and lets out a
soundless roar.

*Save it. You don't have time to be a drama queen. So
pull yourself together and get on with it!*

As if she were physically present in the room—
and not just a voice from the past in his head—he
nods resolutely to his ex-wife. Then he picks up the
last papers, looks them through ... and throws
them back on the table with a sigh.

Weighed down by helplessness, he turns away
from the desk and walks over to the chair, where he
lifts up the clothes and checks below. He knows it's
a long shot, and he's not surprised either, when the
result is the same. Nothing.

He has the same expectation when he, on an impulse, decides to check behind the open door before leaving the office. However, this turns out to
be a good choice, because on the wall behind the
door is a coat rack, and on it hangs a white coat.

In itself, the lab coat isn't very interesting, but
the object sticking out of its pocket may just turn
out to be.

A small, old-fashioned tape recorder. The type
that before the Collapse was used by doctors and
lawyers to dictate messages that their secretaries
would later type down. And which some doctors
have apparently gone back to using now.

Aware that it's probably another long shot, Randall pulls the tape recorder out of the lab coat, lifts it up to his ear, and presses the *Play* button.

"It's 2:24 p.m.," Walker's voice says in the small speaker. "Today is the ... thirteenth, and the results of the first test with live hosts and parasites have just come through the door. It looks promising. All of Derrick's calculations held true, meaning that we now know for certain that the radius of the parasites' telepathy is significantly increased by sending a focused electrical current into the anterior cingulate cortex of the host. We also know that the collective consciousness starts diminishing in *all* the parasites within the same radius as soon as the current exceeds fifty milliamps. And if my theory about Billy Morgan is correct ... well, then this could potentially be the key to destroying the hive mind on a large portion of them simultaneously, taking away their ability to communicate with each other. If we can get a hold of the boy, that is."

There's a click, a short-lived, scratchy noise, and then another click. After that, Walker's voice returns.

"Today is the seventeenth, it's 10:14 p.m., and I'm tired. Tired in my body, tired in my soul. Just *tired*. Why? Because all the samples show the same. Apparently, there is no way to destroy the parasites' hive minds without killing the host. Oh yeah, and then maybe also because I've just lied to the host's dad to get him to bring him to me. Fuck. This is the kind of shit that's easy when you get handed a case by your philosophy teacher on campus—kill one and save a million—but when it's suddenly for real, then ... I don't know. But what the heck was I supposed to say? Could I perhaps persuade you to pick up your son so I can fry his brain? Don't worry, it's for a good cause ... oh, I hate this!"

After the last word, the same click as before sounds, but this time Walker's voice doesn't return. Only a faint, crackling noise can be heard in the recorder's speaker.

Randall's quivering thumb finds the *Stop* button, but he doesn't press it down. He just stands there, listening for a continuation that never comes. Episode three, where Walker bursts into laughter and explains how it was all a joke.

But no, when he finally hears a voice, it doesn't come from the tape recorder in his hand, nor is it Walker's. It comes from outside the lab, and it's David's voice.

"Randall! Get out here!"

Randall looks toward the doorway, then over at the coat rack where the lab coat still hangs, and then at the recorder in his hand.

"Randall?"

"I'm on my way!"

And he is ... but he makes a stop on the way to let the tape recorder slip back into its place in the lab coat's pocket—and to cover it with the sleeve so he's sure it can't be seen.

Out in the lab, he finds David and Ollie standing at a glass table, which they lean over as they study the drawing of Billy.

"Ollie knows where Billy is," David says.

"*Thinks*," Ollie corrects him. "I *think* I know where he might be."

He waves Randall over and then points down at the paper.

"I've seen that contraption he's strapped to

before," he says. "It's over in C4. It's a department similar to this one, just with bigger machines."

"How far away?"

"We're in A2 right now," Ollie says, moving his index finger off the paper and over to an invisible map on the table. "So, if this is us, we need to get all the way ..."

The finger wanders, a little farther than Randall cares for, across the countertop before it stops, and Ollie says:

" ... over here."

Randall grinds his teeth together and makes a hissing sound.

"Yep," Ollie says. "And that's not even the worst part."

"Oh, please do tell."

Ollie nods up towards the ceiling, where the muffled commotion can still be heard.

"If we burst in and take your son, we've got *everyone* on our backs. Kids, soldiers, white coats. *Everyone* will be chasing us. So if we're planning on doing that, we're going to have to get away in a hurry afterwards."

"Can we get out over there?"

"There's an exit, yes, but ..."

"But the car is over here," David finishes for him.

"Unfortunately, yeah."

For a while, none of them say anything. Then David nods and clears his throat.

"I'll handle it."

"Handle what?"

"The car," David says. "If Ollie tells me where you get out from C4, I'll make sure that the car is waiting for you."

Randall takes a breath and opens his mouth, but before he has time to say anything, David cuts him off.

"And I don't want to hear that it's too dangerous. Ollie is right. Finding Billy isn't enough. We also need to get him out somehow, and if this is the way to do it, that's what we're doing. I'll get the fucking car. End of discussion."

Ollie juts his lower lip out, then backs up a few steps while looking at Randall as if to say: *Nope, I'm not gonna get involved in that shit. That's your fight, buddy, not mine.*

But Randall hasn't got the strength for that fight. Moreover, he knows from experience that the battle is lost before it's even started when David's voice hits that pitch. So, he simply nods.

"Good," Ollie says. "That's settled, then. The kid picks up the car, we find Billy, and then we're out of here. And you make sure to keep us updated via the walkie, David."

"I will."

"Fine. Then we better hope I'm not wrong and it turns out to be just as empty over in ... wow, I almost forgot."

He slides his hand into his pants pocket, pulls something out, and throws it to David. In the air, Randall can't see what it is, but the rattling sound when David catches them reveals that it's the key chain with the car keys.

"Let's just say Jameson isn't the world champion of frisking," Ollie says, winking at him. "Do you know the way to the surface from here?"

"I should think so."

"Good. What are you waiting for, then?"

For a moment, David looks confused. Then he

pulls his lips up in a faint smile, after which he checks his gun, turns around, and starts running towards the door. Before heading out, though, he glances back over his shoulder, exchanging a solemn nod with Randall.

"I forgot to ask," Ollie says, when David is completely out of sight. "Was there anything useful? In the office, I mean. Did you find anything besides the drawing that we could use?"

Kill one, save a million.

Randall swallows and then shakes his head slowly.

"No, um ... there was nothing."

chapter 25

As they approach Section C4 of the research center, Randall's vision has become so blurred by the flashing red light that it feels like he's slipping in and out of consciousness. Like he's only half-awake, trapped in a daydream where he dashes through one red corridor after another, not getting anywhere.

Yet, despite the drowsy sensation in his head, he is hopeful. There are two reasons for this. Firstly, every step they take in this direction seems to be putting the disturbing sounds of the children's attacks further behind them. Secondly, there are new sounds ahead that seem promising: the clinking of equipment, faint voices speaking—but no screams and no loud bangs.

"If you have more you want to say to David, now is the time to do it," Ollie whispers, pointing. "Once we're through that door, we'll be so close that they'll hear it if we use the walkie."

Randall slows down, pulls out the walkie, and presses the transmitter button.

"David? Are you there?"

The walkie buzzes for a moment with the sound you'd expect to hear from a leaky gas pipe. Then David's voice emerges.

"I'm here."

"Good. Listen, we're going to have to take a break now so they can't hear us, okay?"

"That's fine. I've also run into a group of kids that I need to find a way around."

Long silence.

"How big a group?"

"Nothing I can't handle," David says. "You just focus on your own thing. I've got this."

Randall feels an urge to ask for more details and hear if he needs help, but he reminds himself that David is no longer the scared teenage boy they met at the gas station in Ridgeview.

"Okay. We'll see you outside, then."

"Deal."

Randall releases the send button and hangs the walkie back on his belt. Next, he catches Ollie's eye and signals that he's ready.

Side by side—and both breathing considerably faster than before—they walk over to the door that will lead them into Ward C4.

"Expect resistance," Ollie whispers. "They'll be on high alert, so they're going to shoot first and ask questions later. Got it?"

Randall leans his back against the wall next to the door, holding his gun close to his shoulder with both hands. That's what answer he gives. Also, he doesn't really want to put it into words. Because truth be told, there's a part of him that prefers it the way it is right now. A part of him that hopes to face resistance ... as it could provide an outlet for his high-strung emotions.

Ollie opens the door, looks in, bends down to his knees, and then waves him along.

The semi-dark room behind the door is a lab with four long tables of the type that one would expect to see in a chemistry class at a high school. There are no other people in there, but behind a frosted glass door on one side, they can see indistinct figures wandering by in both directions.

Ollie, still huddled so he can hide behind the tables, leads him to a door on his left.

"It's a chemical depot," he whispers as he pushes the door open, revealing a narrow space with shelves and refrigerators on both sides. "They usually share them between two labs, so we can use them as shortcuts and avoid a few of the hallways."

What would I have done without him? Randall thinks, and instantly he feels a stab of guilt for letting David go alone.

The next room is also a semi-dark laboratory, but where the previous one had rows of tables, the center of this room is occupied by what looks like a transparent, dome-shaped camping tent. In it stands a robotic arm and a tall cylinder full of test tubes.

What the hell do they mix in a thing like that?

"You really don't want to know," whispers Ollie, who has apparently read the question in Randall's eyes—and he's probably right.

Following the depot shortcuts, they manage to sneak unnoticed through two more semi-dark laboratories, and as they move through the third, Randall starts to think that they actually might have a chance to get all the way to Billy without being seen.

At least up until the moment when he accidentally bumps his arm against a Bunsen burner, so it tips over the edge of the table and falls to the floor.

"Fuck! " Ollie exclaims. "Get to cover! Now!"

Randall throws himself to the floor and only just manages to get behind one of the tables before he hears one of the doors getting ripped open.

For a few nerve-wracking seconds, it's completely silent. Then a click sounds, and the lab is filled with a blueish light that, after so long a time in the semi-darkness, feels like a blowtorch to his eyes.

"Norris! Get off your ass and come over here!"

"What?"

"I heard something."

"Again? You think maybe you should cut back on the coffee?"

"Just get over here!"

No answer, but the sound of footsteps indicates that Norris is following his colleague's orders and joining him in the doorway.

Randall looks down at the gun in his hand, but immediately feels something touch his arm. He lifts his gaze and sees Ollie shaking his head slowly.

After a moment of silence, the sound of shoe soles on linoleum returns. Only this time they are coming from inside the lab and not from outside in the hallway.

On the wall in front of him, Randall can follow the two men's shadows as they move through the lab. Depending on where they are in relation to the light sources—two rows of neon tubes in the ceiling—the shadows shift between being sharp and being blurry, but one fact is certain: they are constantly growing larger. Which means they're getting closer.

Randall peeks down at his gun again, tightens his grip on it—and this time Ollie doesn't shake his head. He does the same.

"I'm afraid you've gotten a bit paranoid in your old age," one of the guards says somewhere on the other side of the table. "There's no one here."

"I *heard* a sound."

"Mm. It couldn't have just been your nerves?"

"What if it's the kids, huh? We know they'll try to get him at some point."

"The kids? Didn't you see Walker's screens? You think they come bursting in like a fucking tsunami over in A, burning shit and stabbing people to death ... but over here, they're going to sneak in like ninjas? Christ! When they come, I think we'll know."

"Yeah, yeah, whatever. I just wish Walker would quit dragging it out and get it over with. Up to full strength and sauté that little shit, if you ask me."

"Oh, come on. You know damn well why they haven't turned it up yet."

"Yeah, but do you really want to tell me that you're not the least bit worried?"

"About what? The kid?"

"No, damn it! That we're the ones who will pay

the price for them stalling, just so they can increase the radius a bit and have a bigger barbecue party."

"Not really."

On the other side of the table, Randall exchanges a glance with Ollie, mimicking the words: *What do we do?*

Ollie closes his eyes and bows his head. When he lifts it again, his eyes are wide open, and he nods solemnly.

Randall nods as well. Then he lifts up his gun with one hand and grabs the edge of the table above him with the other.

Ollie mirrors this movement, and as they both squat down, ready to jump, Randall mimics another silent message.

Three ... two ...

He is interrupted by Ollie, who with a shaking hand points to the back wall.

Randall looks and lets out a sigh of relief. The shadows are getting smaller. The guards are leaving.

As an extension of this thought, a click sounds, and all the ceiling lights go out.

"That was close," Ollie whispers when they are sure that the two soldiers have left the room. "And what was that radius thing they were raving about?"

"No idea," Randall lies. "How far are we from the finish line?"

"Not far. We have to cross one hallway to get over there, but that's it. And if we make sure to avoid more patrols, like those two clowns, it shouldn't be a problem."

"Then let's not waste time," Randall says, pushing himself up. "I've got a feeling we're running short."

chapter 26

As Randall nudges the door open and looks out at the last obstacle—the wide hallway between them and their destination—he realizes that Ollie was mistaken. Patrolling guards pose neither their only nor their biggest problem. That would be the guard sitting on a chair next to the door into the room where Billy most likely is kept.

"How do we get past that guy?"

"Let me have a look," Ollie says, leaning closer to the crack between the door and the frame. After a moment, he leans back, nodding to himself. "That's Nichols. We can handle him. He is what we call a cardboard tiger. Looks dangerous, but tilts over at a gust of wind."

He leans forward again, casting another glance

out through the crevice.

"Here's what we'll do," he then says. "I'll get him over here, and then you'll take David's role this time."

For a moment, Randall doesn't understand what Ollie means, but then he remembers. Ollie wants him to hide behind the door and assault the guard, just like David did down in the cell.

"Fine by me, but how do you plan on getting him in here?"

"Sometimes you don't have to think too much," Ollie says as he pushes himself up from the floor and then opens the door another four to five inches so he can stick his head out.

"Psst! Hey, Nichols."

"Ollie? I thought you were—"

"It was a misunderstanding," Ollie interrupts, and before Nichols gets the chance to say or ask anything else, he adds: "But listen, I was asked to come get you. The kids have breached through in both A and B, so we need all hands on deck to keep them from getting in here."

As he speaks, he waves his hand behind his

back, motioning Randall to get in place behind the door.

"I ... okay, give me a minute so I can let Walker and Andrews know," Nichols says. "They're going to—"

"Sorry, I can't give you that," Ollie says, whereafter he opens the door almost all the way and makes a sweeping motion towards the lab. "We really need to get going. Otherwise, it may be too late."

Nichols doesn't answer, but Randall can hear him getting up from the chair and jogging toward Ollie.

He turns the gun in his hand so he can use it as a club, and when Nichols has gotten far enough into the room, he takes the swing.

The gun's handle hits Nichols in the back of his head with the sound of a chestnut bursting in an oven, sending him stumbling forward.

For a second Randall's inner eye shows him Nichols falling headfirst into the table, taking a bunch of lab equipment with him in the fall, so the entire wing will be warned of their presence ... but then Ollie quickly turns on his heel and grabs the man.

"Like a light," Ollie says. "But we can't be sure how long he'll be out, so … so you go ahead and get over there while the coast is clear. I'll find something to tie him up with and join you when it's done."

Randall hesitates, but only for a fleeting moment before he accepts the deal with a nod, then turns around and walks out of the lab.

Out in the hallway, there is no one in sight in either direction, so he heads straight over to the door that only a moment ago was guarded by the man he just left unconscious.

And seeing Nichols' chair spurs an idea in Randall's mind. He grabs the armrest of the chair with his left hand and pulls it with him, as he uses his right hand—the one holding the gun—to push the door handle down.

The door begins to swing open, and he helps it on its way with a well-placed kick, after which he enters the room with the gun raised.

273

chapter 27

"WHAT HAVE YOU DONE TO HIM?" Randall hears himself shout in a voice that sounds as if the world has finally squeezed the last drop of sanity out of him. Which, in a way, it has. "STEP AWAY FROM THAT ... THING!"

The *thing* is a large control panel with buttons and handles that stands on a raised platform on one side of the room, along with the three people that Randall's outburst is aimed at.

These three people are now staring at him with confusion and fear in their eyes. Two of them he already knows, Walker and Andrews, but the third he hasn't seen before. However, the white lab coat gives away that it must be one of Walker's colleagues.

"I SAID STEP AWAY FROM IT!"

This time, they obey and pull away from the panel with their hands raised, after which they back down the two steps of the platform.

"Randall, before you do anything rash, please listen to me," Walker tries, but Randall silences her by shaking his head.

"I've heard enough of your lies," he says, as he—without moving neither his gaze nor the gun's sight from them—wedges the chair he brought in under the doorknob so the door can't be opened from the outside. "It's your turn to listen to me. Is that clear?"

He lets the question hang in the air as he moves the gun slowly from side to side so all three of them feel the gravity of having it pointed at them—and when he's received a nod from everyone, he points it back at Walker.

"Excellent. Here's what's going to happen. You two stay right there and keep calm while Helen shows me how to turn off this thing. In return, I'll walk out of here without shooting anyone—and I'm taking *him* with me."

As he says the last words, he points the finger of

his free hand towards a large window in the wall behind the top edge of the control panel.

Behind its glass is Billy. He's strapped to a large, slanted plate with leather bands around his wrists and ankles, as if he were a violent patient in an asylum.

Just like the boy from the drawing in Walker's office, Billy has two small, white circles—which Randall now knows are electrodes—sitting on his forehead. From these hang a couple of thin cables that go into a box, which is undoubtedly connected to the control panel on this side of the glass.

As he stands there studying his son, Randall catches a detail he didn't see before. One that makes his stomach tighten.

Billy's small, pink fingers and toes are moving. In small, convulsive jerks, they bend and stretch ceaselessly.

It's the electricity, Allie says in the back of his mind. *You knew it before you walked in here.*

True. But to see it with his own eyes. To see Billy's hands contract in uncontrolled spasms like that ... *nothing* could have prepared him for that.

"We can't, Randall," Walker says. "We can't let you take him. There's too much at stake."

"He's my son," Randall replies, as if that's the definitive answer to anything Walker could think of to say—which isn't far from the truth.

"I know. But you're not thinking clearly right now."

"Show me how to turn it off."

"Think about what it is you're doing. We have the chance to cut off our enemy's ability to communicate through their collective consciousness. Think about how many lives that would save. How many innocents—"

"SHOW ME HOW TO TURN IT OFF!"

His roar causes Walker to jolt in fear, ejecting a faint cry.

She looks over at her colleagues and receives a conceding nod from both.

Slowly, she walks back to the stairs and steps up onto the platform, while Randall, on his side, does the same.

When they've come all the way up to the panel, Walker points to a knob at the top.

"That's the one regulating the current. If it's turned all the way to the left ..."

She hesitates, then turns her face and stares at him with her pleading, hazel brown eyes.

"It's working," she says. "Everything about our theory held true—and the last step would have too. They would still be aggressive, but we would have taken away their ability to communicate."

Randall's throat tightens ... but he doesn't lower the gun.

"I ... I just thought you should know," Walker says, taking a deep breath and a step backward.

As she does this, he catches her squinting over to a wheeled table next to the platform. On it stands a black-and-white monitor of the same type as the ones in the armory. However, this screen only shows the feed from one surveillance camera—which appears to be located in the hallway in front of the room, warning the people in here if the children should get too close.

"If it's Nichols you're looking for, he's taking a nap," Randall says, pointing at the chair under the doorknob. "That was his."

Walker's mouth says nothing. Her eyes, on the other hand, are eagerly trying to set him on fire.

"Was it this one?" he asks, pointing over to the dial.

Walker nods and opens her mouth but is interrupted by two loud beeps from the walkie-talkie on Randall's hip. In their wake follows the sound of David's voice.

"Randall, are you there? Come in!"

Randall can almost physically feel the tense stares of the three hostages resting on him as they wait to see what he's going to do.

"Randall, come in. I need help!"

Anyone else. Had it been anyone else in the whole world, he would have ignored that call without hesitating for a second, but ...

"I'm here, David. What's going on?"

"Oh, thank God. I'm trapped in the freight elevator, Randall. There are kids everywhere. I had to hit the emergency stop button, but that only made it worse because now I'm stuck here and I can, oh fuck, I can hear them above me."

"Okay," Randall says, trying to sound calm. "Let

me just think. Is it the same elevator as the one we normally use?"

"Yeah, the freight elevator."

Randall points his gun at Andrews and then at the monitor on the table.

"Can it show other cameras? Can it show the ones outside?"

"I ... I think so," Andrews stammers.

"Then what are you waiting for? The surveillance camera up by the freight elevator. Now!"

Andrews tilts his head as if the words were actual physical objects flying toward him. Then he jogs over to the monitor and presses a button on its side repeatedly until the desired image appears.

David was right. In front of the elevator stands a group of children. Two of them carry a long object that they're trying to wedge in between the doors. The screen's gritty resolution and the lack of colors make it difficult to see, but it looks like a metal pipe of some kind.

"I see them now, David. We have a feed from a surveillance camera outside. They look like they're trying to break the door open."

"Fuck, Randall," David says. "If they succeed, then ... I think they're planning to cut the wire."

For a split second, Randall envisions that scenario; David, crashing to his death, trapped in a steel coffin, unable to escape.

And that split second Walker takes as her chance to sprint back up the stairs to the control panel.

chapter 28

More than anything, it's a reflex that causes Randall's finger to pull the trigger and fire the bullet that hits Helen Walker in the stomach, causing a burgundy red rose to appear on the white fabric of the lab coat.

Stunned, he stares at her as she staggers backwards, then stumbles on the edge of the steps and tumbles down the stairs.

As she hits the floor, Andrews and the man in the white lab coat instinctively take a few steps forward, but then they both stiffen and cast a nervous glance up at Randall.

He gives them permission with a nod, and as soon as they've gotten it, they both kneel next to their wounded colleague.

Walker is still conscious, but her eyes are foggy and wet. She's clearly struggling to keep them open.

"I ... had to," he stammers.

Walker's gaze flickers feverishly around the room, as if she's having trouble identifying where the sound of his voice is coming from. Then she finally manages to focus on him, and she pulls her lips up in a strained smile.

"So did I," she says.

For a couple of long seconds, Randall is unable to do anything but stare at her as her well-chosen words drop into one of the two scales of his conscience and press it down.

However, before he has time to read the balance, he is interrupted by the walkie, once again beeping on his hip. Right after, David's voice—hollow and discouraged—returns.

"Randall?"

"I'm here."

A long pause.

"I ... I don't think I'm going to make it. There's a grate up in the ceiling of the elevator, and I can see a narrow ray of light farther up in the shaft. I think it's them. I think they've gotten the doors nudged open."

"Of course you'll make it, David."

He would like to say something more, elaborate with just the right words that both comfort and re-assure, but nothing pops up in his head.

Something else does, however, when he turns his face away from the walkie in his hand—and sees his son behind the glass of the window.

"Is he ... can he hear me?" he asks, looking down at the man in the white lab coat who is still kneeling next to Walker.

"Possibly," says the man in the white coat. "He's not fully sedated, because then the electricity wouldn't be able to amplify his signal, but ... I don't know. There's a microphone into the room on the panel."

Randall nods and turns around so he's facing the panel and the window behind it. Next, he locates the microphone, leans forward, and presses its but-ton.

"Billy? Can you hear me? It's Dad."

No response.

"If you can, Billy, then I need you to contact the kids who are chasing David and tell them to stop."

Silence.

"You hear me, Billy? You have to get them to stop. Make them leave him alone."

With each word, Randall's windpipe narrows further so they only barely can be forced through in the end.

And the next words—the ones he now realizes he has to utter—don't make it any easier. Because they are the hardest ones he's ever had to say.

"You have to stop them, Billy," he says, closing his eyes. "If not ... if not I'll turn the dial myself."

For a moment, there is nothing but silence. Then the answer comes, brutal and overwhelming as a tidal wave invading his mind and drowning out all other thoughts.

No, Dad. You won't.

"Billy? Oh God. Don't make me do this. I'm begging you."

I'm not forcing you to do anything. I don't have to. We both know you're not going to turn that dial.

"I'm serious, Billy. I'll turn up the power if you don't let him go."

Even if you wanted to, you couldn't do it. You'd rather let David and all the others die than kill me. It's in your DNA. And why? Because you're my dad ... and a father won't sacrifice his son, no matter the cost.

Through a veil of tears, Randall looks up at the boy behind the glass as his hand moves across the control panel.

"You're right," he whispers, as he grabs the dial and twists it to the right. "No father would willingly sacrifice a son."

chapter 29

When the boy's fingers finally stop quivering and fold together like the legs of a dying insect, Randall's body does the same. The last vestiges of strength and willpower run out of him like water in a dark drain, and he collapses helplessly on the platform floor in front of the panel.

There he sits with his hands clasped in his lap, rocking aimlessly back and forth, encircled by a world that feels more like an abstract idea, a lie, than anything real.

"Hello? Randall, are you still there? Something has happened to the children. They're not up at the door anymore, and ... I don't know why, but a lot of the noise has stopped. Almost no one is shooting anymore."

As he sits there, the walkie's speaker is no more than eight inches from Randall's face. Nevertheless, David's voice sounds as if it's coming from the bottom of a deep well.

"Come in, Randall. Are you there?"

Randall doesn't respond. Not to David's question and not to the two loud, metallic blows sounding from the door behind him. With the drowsy state he is in right now, it's nothing more than irrelevant background noise.

So are the subsequent sounds of voices behind his back. One of them is Ollie's, he perceives this peripherally, but what they are talking about doesn't matter.

In fact, nothing does.

Kill one, save a million. You did the right thing, Randall.

Something grabs his arm, pulls on it. He tries to resist, but can't find the strength, and before he knows it, he's been pulled to his feet.

"It's over," Ollie's voice says so close to his ear that his brain can't dismiss it as being background noise. "Hold on to me, okay? I'll get us out of here.

Do you still have the walkie?"

Without waiting for an answer, Ollie snatches the walkie from Randall's hip and presses the button.

"David?"

"Ollie? Man, you have no idea how happy I am to hear your voice. I thought you were ... hey, wait. Where's Randall? Is he okay?"

"He's with me," Ollie replies. "Where are you?"

"I'm out of the elevator, and I just got to the car. Are you guys out yet?"

"Not yet, but we're on our way."

As Randall listens to the conversation, he sees the floor start to move under him on the other side of the foggy veil of grief. He tries to get his feet to keep up, so Ollie doesn't have to carry all of his weight, but most of the time he ends up hanging like dead weight on his shoulder.

Walls, floors, windows, and flickering red lamps glide by at the edge of his field of vision, and then, all of a sudden, they stand in front of a large, silvery sliding door.

A faint rumble, followed by the sound of a bell,

and the doors open.

The light inside the elevator is overwhelmingly bright, and Randall feels an instinctive resistance toward stepping in there. He tries to let go and back away, but Ollie drags him along—and he doesn't let go until the doors have closed behind them.

When the elevator reaches the top level, its doors slide open again and a chilly wind caresses Randall's face, tries to dry the tears on his cheeks.

It's dark out there. The only source of light is the headlights on the car, from which David now steps out and runs to meet them.

Hopefully that's enough.

part 5

THE BUMBLEBEE

"That it goes on. Yeah, that must be it.
That no matter how hard we kick and scream,
it always goes on."
—O. E. Geralt, Somebody Get This Man!

Epilogue

Spring has come to East Alin, and nature has never been stronger. Green hedges, shrubs, and creepers eat off the facades of houses and the tiles of sidewalks with a ravenous appetite. Dandelions break up through the asphalt of the roads, proudly rising to show off their golden crowns.

It's on one of these crowns that the bumblebee makes its first stop of the day. It lands gently on the thin petals, crawls around a bit to find the best spot, and then sucks in a mouthful of nectar.

As it takes off again, it flies across the road, in through a hole in a faded fence, over a yellow sea of dead grass, past a rusty swing set, and onto a new asphalt road.

Had the bumblebee been able to read, the signs

would have told it that this road is called Saxton Road, and it would also know that the large building with all the windows that it passes is the Hillmore Center.

But certain things mean diddly-squat to bumblebees—and knowing the name of East Alin's largest shopping center is one of these things. It cares just as little about that as it does about all the dried-out corpses. Both those lying on the ground and the few that still hang from the lampposts.

Next to Hillmore is a construction site with a large, square metal structure at the center—and underneath that structure there is something that does actually pique the bumblebee's interest. Because over time, the sandy soil under the structure has been broken by a handful of small, purple flowers.

After a tour of these, the bumblebee leaves the construction site, pulls upwards, and lets itself be carried on a warm breeze through the deserted and abandoned streets of East Alin.

A quarter of an hour later, the asphalt and the stripes beneath the bumblebee have been replaced with shrubs, hills, valleys, and overgrown fields, and there is only one man-made building in sight: a small farm, located at the end of a dirt road, hidden behind a cluster of pine trees.

Curiosity—and the sweet scent of pears—leads the bumblebee upwards along a tree in the farm's garden and from there onto the roof of the house, where it takes a well-deserved break.

As the bumblebee sits there, a loud bang sounds, causing the tile below it to vibrate. Then another.

The sound comes from the hammer that David Pearson is using to pound nails into the new boards he's putting up in the gable.

There are plenty of these kinds of small DIY projects on a run-down building like this—especially if their plan to turn Tommy's old home into a new one for other survivors is to be implemented.

Luckily, David has had an excellent teacher in Randall. He has shown him all the little tips and tricks that David never got a chance to learn from his real father.

But Randall isn't David's only teacher in the art of small repairs. The other is the man in the light brown overalls, who is standing on a ladder at the bottom edge of the roof, keeping the other end of the boards steady while David hammers the nails in.

That man is Ollie Moses, former U.S. Army corporal stationed at the ARL Research Center in Maryland, now a handyman at the Morgan farm in East Alin, Pennsylvania.

From the roof, the bumblebee flies down along one of the beams supporting the awning of the back terrace and afterwards across the garden grass.

On the way, it passes an animal with a bushy tail and reddish fur—and the bee may have gotten a little too close, for the animal is startled and rushes up a tree to hide.

Some distance behind the garden is a clearing, enclosed by an uneven semicircle of pines. In the center of the clearing there are three grave sites, each one marked with a wooden cross.

Although all three crosses bear names, only one of the tombs actually contains the bodily remains of the deceased, while the other two merely serve as memorials.

The memorial graves bear the full names of the people whom they honor, *TOMMY MORGAN* and *ROSE LAVINE*, while the inscription on the cross at the actual tomb consists of only one word.

BILLY.

That the boy could be buried there is solely due to Ollie, who, on the day after the fateful night when the dial was turned, went back to ARL to submit his resignation—and to retrieve the boy's remains so his father could be allowed to give him a proper burial.

And for that, Randall Morgan, who is currently kneeling in front of the grave, is eternally grateful to him.

At least once every day, Randall sits in the same place. It's been like that for the last four months, and it's probably going to be that way for the rest of his life.

At first, it was hard. Partly because of the grief and the shame, of course, but also because it was all still so recent that the memory of Billy was often overshadowed by the memory of the evil that had taken residence in him.

Thankfully, time has made it a bit easier, and Randall has also realized—and *almost* accepted in his heart—that he made the right choice that day. For the world *has* been changed for the better, and the survivors *have* been given a second chance.

Sure, the kids are still out there, and it would be a lie to claim they've become harmless, but their ability to work together, to coordinate and plan attacks, has been taken away. The threads of their shared consciousness have been torn apart, and that has—at least in the southwestern part of Pennsylvania and a decent part of Maryland—reduced them to scattered strays who only show aggression as long as they have their prey in sight.

So yes, Randall did make the right choice, and if over time he comes to accept it fully, that's good ... and if not, then that's okay too. For now, he's just happy that he's starting to appreciate the small joys and find highlights in the days, however small they may be.

One of these highlights occurs in this particular moment, when the bumblebee buzzes past Randall's ear and then lands on the wooden cross at

Billy's grave.

He holds his breath, watching it as it crawls in small circles over the inscription, as if it's trying to read the letters—and when it stops and wiggles its head like it's too much of a challenge, he can't hold it in anymore. He smiles and he cries at the same time.

Very carefully, he reaches out his hand and places the tip of his index finger on the rough surface of the wood, right in front of the bumblebee.

For a moment, it stays perfectly still, perhaps considering. Then it climbs onto his fingernail, staying there as he lifts it up.

What he whispers to the little bumblebee as they sit there is between him and it ... but know that he gets to say what he wants to say.

And when it leaves him again, he's not sad. For he knows that life goes on, and he knows that little miracles like this will continue to appear every now and then ... and that other bumblebees like this one will continue to fly off on adventures.

Even when the world around them tries to tell them that they can't.

this is
THE END

Thanks to ...

Sarah Jacobsen, who is my eternal first reader and my co-conspirator in this life.

Adrian & Sofia Jacobsen, who inspire me every day with their goodness and their exuberant wit.

Kaare & Karina Bertelsen Dantoft, who once again have been an invaluable team to draw upon.

McKenna Rice, who is a fantastic proofreader and editor. I am so grateful to have found her.

Last—but never least—I owe a huge thank you to you, **dear reader**. Our time is precious, and I thank you from the bottom of my heart for yours.

—Per Jacobsen

Milton Keynes UK
Ingram Content Group UK Ltd.
UKHW041135061024
2026UKWH00022B/57

9 788794 319065